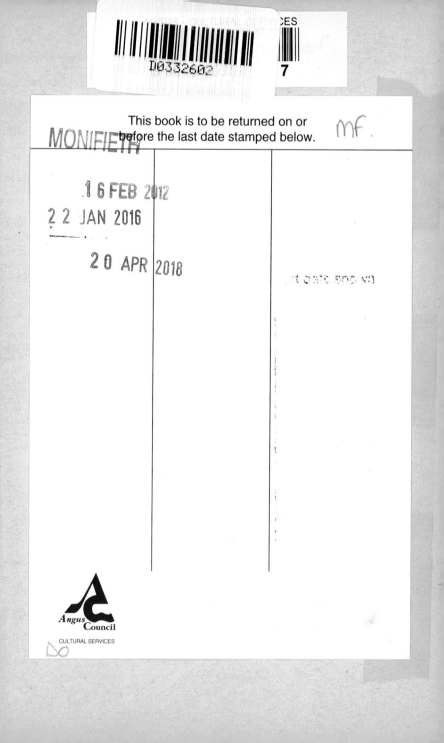

Burning Mountain

L. J. ADLINGTON

Hodder
Children's
Books

A division of Hachette Children's Books

First published in Great Britain in 2010
by Hodder Children's Books

1

A Catalogue record for this book is available from the British Library

ISBN: 978 0 340 95682 3

Typeset in Berkeley Book and Frutiger by Avon DataSet Ltd,
Bidford on Avon, Warwickshire

Printed and bound in Great Britain by
CPI Bookmarque Ltd, Croydon, Surrey

The paper and board used in this paperback by Hodder Children's Books
are natural recyclable products made from wood grown in
sustainable forests. The manufacturing processes conform to the
environmental regulations of the country of origin.

Hodder Children's Books
a division of Hachette Children's Books
338 Euston Road, London NW1 3BH
An Hachette UK company
www.hachette.co.uk

For Mr Plumpton

An excellent man and an extraordinary teacher

To be ignorant of what occurred before you were born is to remain always a child.

Marcus Tullius Cicero

On the Beach

AD79

Drenched in grey ash, grazed by a rain of rock, Gaius Justinius Aquila staggered along the beach, eyes wide at all the horrors.

Boiling sea. Savage sky. Burning mountain.

Children stood and screamed.

Fingers clawed his arm, a slave girl with a baby, crying, 'I don't want to die! Tell me what to do!'

'How can I know? Get away from me!'

He limped to an ash-grey shape at the water's edge. Praise the gods – a slender wooden boat with one oar still inside.

Now he was seized by a woman in a saffron yellow gown.

1

'Help me, soldier! I'll give you everything, my jewels, the rings on my fingers, here, take them now . . . Just row me across the bay, I'm *begging* you!'

'Hush, woman! There's only one boat and no room for all these hundreds . . .'

Too late. A crowd closed round him. Desperate men and women with wild eyes. No time to draw his sword. They tore the oar from his hands and launched the boat without him, flinging themselves inside at the last moment.

One surge later it was hurled back on shore. Empty.

Still the children screamed.

He turned his back on their pale faces. He was one man, they were many. How could he help?

The sky collapsed into thick, choking darkness.

Did he turn again at the moment of death?

When the blast came his life burned away and his body was stamped flat on the sand.

Unexpectedly Criminal

All old people are loons. They can't help it. Nice but nuts, that's what I think.

Take the old lady next door. We only went round because it was an emergency. I knocked. A light came on. A spindly shadow showed behind the door glass. Craig wanted to wimp out but I yanked him back to my side. Safety in numbers.

She was tall, with clouds of white hair floating round her face, and sharp, dark eyes. She kept the chain on the door, as if we were about to shove our way in and rob her blind. At a glance there didn't seem to be anything worth nabbing in her kitchen, just margarine-tub towers and yellowy magazines. Oh, and the eight shiny bullets lined up on the spice rack next to the door. By the time I spotted those it was too late to escape so I smiled and said, 'Sorry to bother you, Miss.'

'It is *Doctor*, not Miss. Doctor Shepherd.'

'Sorry . . . Doctor. I'm Denise Cooper from next door. This is my little brother Craig.'

'You appear wet.'

'It's raining.'

'Then you are silly to stand in the rain with no coats. What a shame when you catch pneumonia and drop dead.'

'Look,' I said slowly. 'I've left my key at school and Craig's lost his again, and we just need to borrow a phone to call our mum at—'

'At the hospital, where she works. Yes, I saw her go in her nurse's uniform. You young people have those mobile things, yes? No?'

Me and Craig swapped looks. We both got phones last Christmas. We're both out of credit. The door closed. I slumped.

Plan B was to go shelter at the bus stop on the end of the street and hope we didn't freeze to death, but then the chain rattled, the door opened again and Dr Shepherd came out wearing a waterproof tent-coat-thing and a hat with a ten-mile brim. She dived straight into the hedge struggling to grow between her house (sixty-four Willow Garth) and ours (sixty-two). She explained that she always took this short cut when Winnie escaped into our garden.

Craig pulled at my sleeve. 'Who's Winnie?'

No idea.

Like idiots we tried the short cut too, getting wet twigs stuck in our jumpers, our hair, our faces . . . Dr Shepherd didn't take the blindest bit of notice. She put an odd piece of metal in the keyhole of our back door and wiggled it gently.

'Your mother gives me no key so I cannot even feed your fish when you are away. Stupidity when people do not help each other!'

Craig said, 'We don't know any of our neighbours. This street's just boring.'

'What do you want?' she snapped. 'A war in your back garden, or a volcano perhaps? Now, sss! I concentrate. Once I could do this with closed eyes, but now, look! It is impossible – already there is a key in the lock, inside.'

He confessed, 'I must've left it there this morning so I wouldn't forget it.'

Dr Shepherd carried on jiggling at the keyhole but the key wouldn't fall out. She tried reaching up through the cat flap, but it was locked because we don't have a cat. She asked if we had a key to the front door instead, which made sense. So much sense I would've thought of it myself. Eventually. Except there was no key to the front door.

And that's when she did it. The old bat wrapped her fist in her woolly scarf and *smashed* the door glass. Actually broke into our house! She just reached through the jagged hole and turned the key, saying, 'You may go in now. Please, don't believe neighbours will telephone the police. They are all watching bad programmes on television. Everyone busy busy with their lives.'

Oh well that's all right then. My hands itched for a phone. Who would I call if I could – the cops or the docs at the mental hospital?

She warned, 'Watch your step.'

Too late for my klutz-R-us brother. He pushed into the hall and skidded on a large shard of broken glass. His arms flailed, just like on the cartoons, as he reached for something other than thin air to hold on to, only there wasn't anything except old phone books and photos and the big fish tank. To be fair, he did try and catch the fish, tricky at the best of times, more so when you're falling backwards under a flood of water and weed. He slashed his skin. Swore. Apologised for swearing.

I reached in to flick the light switch. The bulb sparked once and went out. It was a perfectly natural reaction to shriek aloud. Anyone would've done the same in my position.

Dr Shepherd told me to use her torch and get the washing-up bowl, quickly. I worked out for myself it needed filling with water. Running the tap at top gush I could still hear her chattering on.

'Fish are funny animals, flap flap flap out of water. Enough for a mouthful. Nice with chips. Here is the last one – swimming in a shoe. Craig, stop bleeding on the carpet!'

He wailed, 'It hurts!' and that nearly made me forget the fish and call an ambulance to rush him to A&E.

What Dr Shepherd said next left me speechless. Real speechless, when you don't actually say anything, not when you gabble on and on like actors winning an award. Here's what she said: 'Hurts? Not as much as when your leg is blown off by a landmine.' These were her exact words.

I thought of Richard. Stopped thinking of Richard. Went looking for a first-aid kit. Remembered Mum had it in the car from when we last went on a trip to the seaside – in the days when she still had time for trips. The car was at the hospital. Should I rip my school shirt up to make a bandage? Better idea – use a tea towel.

Craig brushed me off. 'It's all right. Just a scratch. I'm going down the garden.'

'Why?'

'Miss . . . I mean, Dr Shepherd wants to know if we've got a hammer. There's Rich's tool kit in the shed.'

You could practically see the old lady's ears sit up and beg for gossip. 'Richard – your brother? The paratrooper?'

How did she know that?

Next thing, she'd picked the lock on the shed door and was merrily nailing a square of wood into place over the broken glass of our back door. I had to admit I was impressed with her DIY skills – something we don't see a lot of at our place – so when she told me to put the fish down and come to her place to get dry I sort of found myself being meek and going, 'If it's really no trouble . . .'

To be fair I did take a nanosecond to review the situation:

Item 1. Cold, dark, autumn afternoon? *Check*

Item 2. Central heating still bust, fridge empty and house freezing? *Check*

Item 3. Feel like have been flushed down a toilet? *Check*

Item 4. Great excuse to avoid doing homework? *Absolutely Check.*

Then I noticed Craig going bright red like he was choking only he didn't thank God, but his eyes said *no no no*. I couldn't exactly ask him outright what was wrong in case he said something embarrassing, like the time he was five and I was eight and we were in the newsagent's and he asked, *Mum, why does that hairy lady smell of wee*? So I backtracked a bit with, 'Er perhaps we can just get Mum's key if we walk to the hospital.' Which was miiiiles away.

Dr Shepherd stared at me. 'Stupidity! Get some dry clothes and visit me for hot chocolate, *pronto*.'

As soon as she'd gone Craig pulled me to one side and hissed, 'What about the skull?'

'What skull?'

'The one on her kitchen table.'

'A real one?'

'I just saw it through the open door. Do you think we're gonna get buried under the patio and murdered?'

'Don't you mean murdered *then* buried under the patio?'

'It's bad either way.'

That was true, though it didn't mean Craig was making sense. 'Rain's got in your brain,' I said. 'You're hallucinating. Or mad. Or both. Come on, we never do anything dangerous. Let's give it a go. What's the worst that can happen?'

So we shoved ourselves through the hedge again back to number sixty-four. I suppose that makes both of us loons too.

The old lady was already whisking hot chocolate in a saucepan.

I blurted out, 'There really is a skull on your table!'

She said, 'Ssh! Don't wake Winnie!'

'The skull's called Winnie?'

'No no! But it is a marvellous specimen, yes?'

'It's not real. Is it?'

'Of course it's real. Touch it.'

'No thanks.'

'Was it one of your patients?' Craig asked.

She stared at him as if *he* was the nutter. 'Patience?'

'You being a doctor . . .'

'Oh! Not that sort of doctor. Once I was a lecturer at Cambridge University. Now I am old and can never find teaspoons.'

Apart from the skull, and that easily overlooked row of eight unshot bullets, the kitchen at number sixty-four was pretty much like ours, only warm, dry and light. There was one of those rainbow-coloured plastic strip curtains over the door to the lounge. I could just about see through to a couple of squashy armchairs, a music stand and tons of books.

Dr Shepherd ordered, 'Open the cake tin. Eat, eat! Those round ones, they are almond and marzipan biscuits from Italy. Go on – sit down. I will show you something.'

More skulls? Severed ears? Trophies from former kills?

Nothing so gruesome – just a load of junk wrapped in an old newspaper. I spotted a shabby strip of green cloth embroidered with silver words – an insignia.

'Army stuff,' I said. 'At least, that woolly green thing is.'

Craig perked up. 'Army stuff? The writing's not English. How 'd'you say it, *Fall Sherm Jagger*?'

'Duh! It's German. You say the "J" as a "Y" and the "a" with dots on the top makes it sound like our capital "A".'

'Smart ar— I mean, sorry Dr Shepherd.'

The old lady tutted at him. 'A great philosopher from Roman times said, *Knowledge itself is power*. It is good to know things.'

I told her I was learning German at school and she was impressed. She read out the writing – *Fallschirmjäger Regiment 3* – and explained that *Fallschirmjäger* meant 'parachute hunter', or paratrooper.

'Cool,' said Craig. 'That's what our brother Rich is, except he's not German.'

'The insignia looks old,' I interrupted quickly.

Dr Shepherd touched the silver words gently. 'Oh it certainly is. It was worn in the war.'

11

'Which one?' asked Craig. I knew why. He was thinking of our dad.

Dr Shepherd just snorted and said, 'The Second World War, of course!' as if there hadn't been any others. She added, 'Sadly, the boy who wore this died.'

That was quite enough. You don't talk about soldiers dying in front of two people who've got a big brother serving in a wild part of Afghanistan.

'Ta for the chocolate and thanks for mending our broken door. We're going now. Craig, put the biscuit tin *down*.'

Old people get emotional sometimes. They can't help it. I was almost at the door when, without warning, she gripped my arm really hard. Her words fired out like bullets.

'You must come back soon. You're the only one who can help. Time is running out. Something was taken. It must be returned!'

Like I said, old ladies are loons, only this one looked straight into me when she spoke. If I hadn't known better I'd've said she wasn't mad but desperate.

Audaces Fortuna Iuvat

Craig's science homework was making soda volcanoes, otherwise known as Making A Mess.

'Look!' he squeaked as the whole revolting concoction fizzed out on to the kitchen table, splattering my notebooks. 'It's Vesuvius erupting!'

'I'll erupt you in a minute! Can't you see I'm trying to revise?'

It was a lost cause. I gathered everything up and retreated to my bedroom. Even then I couldn't concentrate, not when I had the old lady's words running round my head.

Time is running out. Something was taken. It must be returned. What exactly did that *mean*?

It bugged me all evening and all the next day, from when we finally escaped from number sixty-four, through

Mum's late-night explosion over the broken door glass, through the grisly episode at breakfast where I poured sour milk all over the last of the cereal, right up to the middle of the afternoon German class when Gavin Parker leaned back in his chair and asked me, *Kommst du mit ins Kino?* and all I could blurt out was – *Fallschirmjäger!*

There wasn't a whole lot of recovery possible after that, not when my face was sizzling pink with embarrassment. Why am I such I washout? I never manage to do *anything*. I tried to shrug it off, thinking, who'd want to go to the movies with Gavin Parker anyway? The answer: me and just about every other girl in my year.

Cue sick feeling in stomach.

More sick feelings when I twigged it must be the *torch* Dr Shepherd was on about being taken. I'd left it in our kitchen by accident. Fine, I'd go over to sixty-four and give it back.

First I had to give myself a virtual kiss-of-life after the shock of getting home and finding our back door had glass in it again, *and* there was a light bulb in the hall – one of those curly 'green' ones. Aliens had obviously kidnapped Mum and replaced her with someone useful. Or . . . (further sick feelings) . . . the mad lady next door had been do-gooding again.

It must be returned.

14

I postponed hair-tearing-out and shoved through the hedge at top speed.

'Hello. I brought your torch back!'

Dr Shepherd looked confused. 'Oh – keep it, keep it.'

'I thought you . . .'

'Will you come in? Already your brother is here.'

Soundless goldfish impression from me. What was *Craig* doing there?

Lying stretched out on the lounge floor with a plate of hot toast at his side, that's what. Helping him lick crumbs off the plate was a wheezing mutt of a dog so creaky it made Dr Shepherd look pre-teen.

'Look, this is Winnie,' Craig said, with love-hearts in his eyes. 'She likes me!'

The old dog did in fact slobber affectionately on my brother's school jumper. We're not allowed pets, apart from the fish. Mum says we've got to Prove Ourselves Responsible first, which is hardly fair considering we only killed two fish so far, through neglect (or was it overfeeding? Hard to tell without an autopsy). Anyway, the other three were doing fine in the washing-up bowl . . . a great excuse for not doing the dishes.

Winnie thumped her tail on the carpet. Dr Shepherd cleared a space for me on one of the squashy chairs and fetched over a massive slice of chocolate cake. I sat down.

Piles of sheet music slithered off the chair arm on to the carpet.

She said, 'Your brother wanted to see the insignia again.'

'Yeah, it's neat,' he gushed. 'Dr Shepherd says in World War Two German paratroopers had screaming eagles as their symbol, with big claws, like *this*.' He bent his fingers and dive-bombed Winnie's belly. She yipped with happiness.

Dr Shepherd ran her fingers along a row of books and pulled one out. Just to be polite I looked at the picture she showed us. It was a poster showing Craig's eagle hurtling down to grab the slogan, *Mit Unsern Fahren Ist Der Sieg*! Roughly translated by Yours Truly as, *With us goes the something something or other*, or, as the old lady explained: *Victory Follows Our Banners*.

'It is a good picture for recruitment, yes?' she said. 'Many boys wanted to be a *Fallschirmjäger* in those days but only the best were selected. They trained hard. Any sign of weakness, any test failed – out!'

'Just like now,' said Craig. 'My brother Rich says paras are the best of the best.'

She gave him a funny look and nodded. When she spoke next she was . . . I don't know. Relentless? Like she wanted to challenge him.

16

'But these German soldiers were the *bad* guys, you would say. As boys they played in the Hitler Youth, yes, and had Hitler's picture on the wall of their houses. They listened to Josef Goebbels on the radio. That man was a demon for propaganda – at Hitler's side till the very end. He would inflame an army of Nazis screaming, screaming for Total War. *Only Germany can save Europe! Resist the corruption of Jews! Kill the Communists! Und Sturm brich los!* LET THE STORM BREAK LOOSE!'

For a moment I was caught up in the horror and power of the growly words, then I saw the contempt twisting her face. I took comfort from the fact she was wearing a sweater decorated in fluffy sheep, not Nazi swastikas. She softened a bit.

'The *Fallschirmjäger* boys were strong and confident, no weakness, no uncertainty. They wanted to conquer the world! They believed in Germany so much. They were young, of course, so young. One new recruit in 1943, he was only fifteen . . .'

Craig practically hit the ceiling. 'No way!'

I calmly pointed out fifteen was way too early to sign up. Craig bragged he was going to join Richard's regiment as soon as he was old enough. Dr Shepherd raised one eyebrow – a trick I've always envied.

'How old are you, Craig? Ten? Eleven?'

17

'Thirteen.'

I kicked him. Lying is a vice.

'Thirteen in two months,' he muttered.

She said, 'You don't look so old. When I was a girl we would call you a runt. However, being short is useful when avoiding sniper fire.'

'Rich says Afghanistan's crawling with snipers.'

'A hazard of war, yes?'

Then, just when I was revving up to say Enough Talk Of War, Dr Shepherd had the nerve to go and be reasonable, saying war was no place for young people, that even back in Hitler's Germany you were supposed to be seventeen to sign up, and only then with parental permission.

'So how could anyone do it at fifteen?' Craig asked.

'If you want something as much as Peter Schäfer did, you find a way. Have you never forged a signature? Is it difficult? His mother did not object when she knew. She boasted, "My son, fighting for the Fatherland!" He was big, quite mature, not playing computer games all the time.'

'Because they didn't have computers in those days.'

'Because he was doing sport! Always he was running fast, climbing – best at running. Good enough for the Olympics, they said. He came from Bad Kohlgrub, a town in Bavaria, the south of Germany. A nice place if you like beer and mountains and cows with bells on. Boys from Berlin made fun of his accent and his farm life, but he was strong, never lazy. Turnip, they called him, especially his best friend Erich.'

'So this boy just went along and joined . . . ?'

Don't even think it, kiddo.

'Yes he did. As the poet Virgil once said, *Audaces fortuna iuvat.*'

Craig giggled. 'I don't speak Italian except *pizza*.'

'You can hardly manage English,' I said.

'It is not Italian, but Latin,' said Dr Shepherd. '*Fortune favours the bold.* The war was almost three years old when Peter joined, thousands of men had died, thousands more were needed because Hitler was fighting on many fronts. Peter had luck in the recruitment office. Good luck, bad luck – difficult to say. No knowing where he'd be sent of course, not till he arrived. Russia, Greece, France . . . so many countries crawling with Germans! Italy was different. *Ciao, Hitler, welcome to my country*; said Mussolini. What? You haven't heard of Mussolini?'

Were our faces so obviously blank?

'Mussolini was the fascist leader of Italy. *Believe! Obey! Fight*! This was his . . . how do you say . . . propaganda?'

'Slogan?' I suggested.

19

'Yes, his slogan. And he was greedy for countries to conquer too. That man and Hitler, they were cutting up the world like a cake. Would you like some more?'

Cake or conquests? I wondered. Ah. Cake. I couldn't say no.

'Now listen. The Germans were starting to lose battles in 1943, so Hitler wasn't happy.'

'Hitler was evil,' said Craig helpfully.

I groaned, 'Tell us something we don't know!'

Dr Shepherd took me a bit too seriously. 'Something you don't know? Let me see, did you know the volcano Vesuvius erupted during the war? Most spectacular! Very terrible. But! Look at the time. You will have homework, yes?'

'Done it,' we both lied in unison.

'Good students! Your mother works late and my husband is out so I will make us hot dinner and tell you about the paratrooper, if you like.'

I didn't 'like'. Well, I did and I didn't. It felt odd being in her house, surrounded by towering bookcases and photos of black-and-white people. Days aren't supposed to be odd. They're supposed to go one after the other with nothing much happening, except some days it rains and some days it doesn't. Mum works; Mum's at home tired. I go to school, I come home, I watch TV, go to bed, get up . . . What did my life have to do with mad ladies, scruffy dogs and scrappy old insignias?

She started talking again before I could work up the effort to leave. Trouble was, she had the sort of voice that made you listen, especially when you had *time-is-running-out-something-was-taken-it-must-be-returned* running through your head.

'As I said, there was a boy of fifteen years, Peter Robert Schäfer. He was sent to Italy in 1943, to defend it in case the Allies invaded.'

'That's us, right?' asked Craig. 'The English.'

'*British*,' she countered. 'And Americans, and Australians and Indians and New Zealanders and Canadians and Poles and . . .'

'Hold on!' I said, thinking this was getting way out of hand. 'Can I just get this straight? Didn't the Allies invade France, not Italy? We did it at school. D-Day and Normandy, Winston Churchill's *fight them on the beaches* and all that? I never heard about Italy being in the war.'

'Always the television is showing programmes about D-Day! But think of the Mediterranean sea . . .' Dr Shepherd happily knelt on the floor and mussed up a rug into a vague sea shape. 'Look, Europe at the top, Africa at the bottom. Craig, fetch one of my husband's boots from the kitchen. Here, this boot lying on its side is now Italy.

At the toe of Italy I put a teacup – the island of Sicily. The Allies pushed the Germans out of North Africa first, then captured Sicily. What can happen next?'

'They can just hop across to Italy from there!'

'Thank you, Craig. The Allies had to break into Fortress Europe, as it was called. Here, on this curve of the boot here, this is where they were going to land, in the bay of Salerno. Not far north of Salerno are the old Roman towns of Herculaneum and Pompeii . . .'

'Next to Vesuvius!'

Her voice darkened. 'Next to Vesuvius, as you say. Here is Naples, north of Salerno, also along the coast. This is where Peter came first, in July 1943.'

'Is Venice near Naples?' I asked, dredging up the name of another Italian place.

Her look could've cracked concrete.

'Have you been to Italy? No? Nowhere but England? Peter, too, was ignorant like you. It was his first time to leave Germany when they flew, the *Fallschirmjäger*. Of course, no surprise, where there is a boy there is usually a girl not very far away . . .'

'Oh, this isn't going to be a love story, is it?' moaned Craig.

Dr Shepherd laughed.

Glory

July 1943

Erich Bergen said, 'Someone climb up on the roof and tie a swastika round that statue!' So up went Peter Schäfer, bottle of wine in his belt, Nazi flag between his teeth.

Out of the attic window he went, on to the parapet of the old Italian palazzo. Ancient stone crumbled. A couple of tiles jostled. Lead guttering cracked a little more.

'Can you make it?' Erich called.

Stupid question!

Trees, mountains, he could climb anything, do anything. He was a paratrooper. One of the men, right? A proper soldier – gun cleaned, checked, loaded. Knife

23

stowed. Uniform stiff, new, dusty, smart. Eagle on lapels. Hair cropped. Chin nicked – not much to shave yet.

'Does Naples look any better from up there?'

'It could hardly look any worse. Whoa!'

One boot slipped. Peter steadied himself against one of the stone statues posturing on the parapet. He wasn't afraid of falling, or heights, or anything in fact, but it was a long way down to the ground, if someone did fall – someone not so strong and surefooted.

The city spread along the shore of the Mediterranean, streets sinking in darkness, rooftops grazed by the light of a near-full moon. Bomber's Moon they called it, when it was so ripe and white and bright. Domes, towers, tiles, everything looked less derelict at night. Almost impressive. Like being two thousand years back in time, looking out over the once grand Roman town . . .

His neck prickled. He whipped round. Was someone on the roof with him? Eyes and ears keened the shadows. Slowly his gaze was drawn away from Naples to the curve of the bay, dim in the wartime blackout. There the stars had been swallowed by a lump of shadow in the shape of a mountain. Vesuvius! Dormant. Nothing to be afraid of. Not that he was afraid. He wasn't shivering, it was too hot for that.

He jumped as the air growled . . . but it was only an

angry rumble of German tank destroyers passing along the nearby marina, heading south towards where the war would be if the Allies dared invade.

'Save some action for us!' he yelled to the convoy.

The city swallowed his words and their echo.

With one hand he took the wine bottle and prised the cork out with his teeth; with the other he hugged his statue. It was a Roman soldier with thick legs and a shield crusted with dirt. The soldier's face was eroded to a featureless blank.

'*Ave*, Centurion. Hail and well met! You should be glad you have no nose, my friend, because Naples stinks. Smell that rancid olive oil. You can taste the sewerage on your tongue. Not much of a seaside paradise for Caesars now, hey? Look at the place! Except you can't – no eyes. You called us Germans barbarians. Your empire was great but it's long gone. Our turn for glory now.'

He took a swig of wine and laughed to think how angry his father used to get when he sneaked a beer at home. *You smell like a brewery*! his little sister Sophie would screech. Back then one sip would've been enough to earn him a cuff round the ear and a lecture on the evils of alcohol.

Erich's voice broke his memories.

'What are you messing about at, Schäfer? Tie

the flag and come down!'

Peter dutifully wrapped the flag round the statue's neck.

The swastika rippled in a breeze that carried the smell of salt water and the sound of planes approaching, a dull slow drone that made his head throb, or was that the wine? How many bottles had they gone through already? What did it matter? It was their first night abroad. They had every right to celebrate. Corporal Mahler said the regiment could be held in Naples for a week at least, unless fresh orders came. Then maybe they would *fight*, actually get into the war properly.

'Schäfer, you turnip, get back down here! Hey – Peter!'

Who was that calling his name? Didn't they realise he could hardly hear over the engine noise?

He peered over the parapet and spotted Erich's ruff of red-brown hair. 'You look like a squirrel.'

Erich choked. 'Are you deaf?'

'A squirrel with a good aim, I'll give you that. A better shot than me but not as fit and definitely not as fast.'

'Deaf *and* dumb?'

'Just toasting our future glories here in Italy!'

'Yes, yes, medals and honours and as many girls as we can manage before breakfast,' shouted Erich, 'but stop spilling wine everywhere and get down here!'

'You sound like an old woman, scolding.'

A peal of church bells broke the air. Peter checked his watch. Nine o'clock. After nine, in fact. The chimes were wrong. Back home, nine was about the hour Father would say, *That's enough books for one evening, son*, and Mother would put her knitting down and present a powder-floury cheek for the goodnight kiss. *Off you go to bed, school tomorrow.*

Not any more! No school tomorrow!

Clang! Clang! New bells took up the refrain. He blinked some of the wine from his mind and understood. It was an air raid. *That's* what all the fuss was about. He knew what to expect. Although his home town hadn't been hit, he'd seen raids on the flickering news reels at the cinema – cities in Russia and England pulverised by the might of the German air force. Soon there would be searchlights, explosions, fires, ruins . . . But no school, no school ever again!

He'd gone back to school once, when training was over and he was a fully-fledged paratrooper. He went sauntering by his old classroom to show off his uniform to the one teacher who'd been worth listening to.

Professor Meyer was a short man who had to look up at the bigger lads in the class, Peter especially. He said, 'So this is where you've been all this time. I heard you had signed up. All those extra Latin lessons, all that

27

effort cramming words and wisdom into your head and now one bullet will finish it for ever.'

'I am not going to get shot!' Peter tapped the eagle on his lapel. 'See the eagle. *In hoc signo vinces.* You taught me that. *In this sign victorious.*'

Prof Meyer felt around for his spectacles as if cleaning them would help him understand the war better – stupid old man, didn't he realise there would be supreme victory? That all the land lost to the Allies so far would be clawed back and the soldiers would march home singing?

'I am pleased you have remembered something from my lessons, Schäfer. Didn't I also teach you a line from Erasmus? *Dulce bellum inexpertis.* Can you translate that, perhaps, now you know so much?'

Peter shrugged. What use was Latin when you're capable of killing a man with your bare hands?

'Forgotten already? Allow me to remind you: *War is sweet to those who have no experience of it.*'

Experience? What did Meyer know? The war he'd fought in, the Great War, that was old news. *This* was experience, this rooftop in Naples. *This* was living!

'Don't you want me to do my duty, to fight for the Fatherland?' he asked Prof Meyer that time, all the while thinking, how small this classroom is, how shabby, how pointless all the lines on the blackboard are when your head is full of combat tactics and battle commands . . .

'For the Fatherland, yes,' Meyer answered slowly, 'I want ultimate victory – but you are *fifteen*, Schäfer. A schoolboy, not a soldier. To die so young!'

'I have a helmet.'

'You have a death wish!'

Enough talk about dying!

Peter drank in wine and night air, though his ears were ringing from the dang, dang, clang, clang, ring, chime, rhyme of the bells.

Let them ring!

Erich's voice blended with the clamour. 'I'm serious, Schäfer! Get down before I drag you down!'

'In a minute!'

'Not in a minute – *now*!'

Bang, bang, bang, his head was thumping. Were there demons on the ropes of every bell in the city?

He raised the bottle to the heavens.

'In this sign victorious!' he shouted.

As before his words were lost. More was lost with them – a battered red-backed book fell from his pocket and tumbled past the parapet, the attic, the tall windows of dirty glass and further down into the darkness of the narrow street. Squares of paper blew loose from its pages. Faces. Photographs. Loved ones smiling. Pieces of home.

Like a lunatic he forgot everything except the need to catch his diary, reaching down as if he could pluck it out of nowhere, boots slipping, hand slipping, all of him slipping from the parapet ... He clutched at night air. Seized something. The flag. Heard it rip. Someone grabbed him. Shook him. Swore at him. Fondly compared him to every aspect of idiocy since the dawn of time. For a moment he thought it was the Roman soldier stretching out a stone hand to help, then he realised it was Erich, always Erich, ever since the day their scalps were shaved and training began. Utter friends. Mates to the death.

'He's pickled,' said Erich once Peter had been hauled back into the attic.

'He's brought the bottle down in one piece,' said 'Lanky' Lutz Dullman. 'Sit on his chest, Bergen, so I can prise it from his hand.'

'You'll all be sitting on the end of my gun in a minute!' shouted a new voice.

Instant sobriety. Instant attention. Peter was up off the floor and ramrod straight as Corporal Mahler stormed into the attic, slamming the window shutters to hide the glare from their kerosene lamp.

'You know the rules on blackout! We may be billeted in a dump last fit for human habitation in the sixteenth century or God knows when – that doesn't mean I want it demolishing *while I'm still in it*! Enough schoolboy pranks. Get down to the cellars!'

Not a schoolboy, a *soldier*, the voice in Peter's head insisted.

Then the first bombs fell.

Grime and Crime

July 1943

Sunrise.

The light seemed different here by the sea. It hurt.

Peter sat up in his bed-roll and waited for the nausea to pass. As he leaned forward his metal ID tags swayed. He shrugged on his jacket and stepped between the rest of the platoon, all sweaty in sleep. It was hot outside and gritty with dust from last night's raid. What time had the all-clear sounded? He couldn't remember.

Now where the hell was his diary? What an idiot he'd been to lose it, his first day in a new country.

Naples was already awake. He stared at the people who passed along the narrow street. Real foreigners – wait till he wrote and told Sophie about them. Blackshawled matrons lugged baskets bigger than their own bodies. Child-sized rags with arms, legs and wide-eyed heads scampered along, barefoot in the muck. Men too old to fight in the Italian army swayed as they walked, as skinny as skeletons. They all pressed up against the crumbling walls as a German despatch bike churned up the air with fumes and engine revs.

Heil Hitler, Heil Hitler. The locals had learned that much respect, but their voices were faint and their fascist salutes no stronger than limp pasta.

Thank God! The diary was there, where it had fallen, intact and undamaged save for a motorcycle tyre track across the front cover. He looked up to the roof of the palazzo. The faceless stone soldier was brilliant white in the morning sun.

He gathered up scattered photographs and letters, blowing them free of dust.

Mother wrote to him twice a week, on sheets of brown wrapping paper cut into squares, each sentence formed with agonising care, probably with a dictionary close at hand. *Father sends his regards* was always tagged on the last page. Lisa, his girl back home, wrote on thick, watermarked paper. He held one of her notes to his nose, surprised it still had a ghostly scent of flowers.

Erich slapped him on the shoulder.

'You're up early. Quite a firework show last night, eh? Rumour has it bombs took out a few slums in the suburbs. Nothing important. Americans can't aim to save their lives. Mahler says we muster at eight for more kit inspection. What's that? A *school* book? The Turnip can read? Is this your scribbling in the margin?'

'It's private.'

Erich grinned and pretended to decipher the pencil words wrapped around printed paragraphs of text.

'*Dear Diary, Today I am in Italy and it is hot so I'm going to buy my friend Erich a beer for breakfast . . .* Your handwriting is appalling. What's all this other stuff? Italian?'

'Latin. It's just an old textbook.'

Erich pounced on one photo in particular. 'Who is *this* foxy lady?'

'Lisa. I told you about her.'

'I thought you were making her up.'

'Like all *your* girlfriends?'

'And we were all saying she'd be some sort of dumpling in peasant costume.'

Peter wrestled him for the diary and jammed it into the front pocket of his combat trousers, tossing Erich's cap up on to a shop awning in retaliation. Erich used his rifle butt to knock the cap free. A few more soldiers spilled out into the sun. Lanky Dullman with his shambling walk – too tall to realise what his feet were up to, everyone joked. Heini Holz, serious, efficient, humour as dry as the desert. Joseph 'Jupp' Weiss, eyes darting this way, that way, already shuffling a pack of cards. Good lads, all of them.

Peter followed everyone to a dingy café on the marina, nowhere near as nice as the neat beer cellars back home in Bavaria, he thought. The tables set outside were warped and stained. The chairs had splinters and spindly legs. They'd do.

He nudged Erich. 'Look, there are lemons growing on those trees.'

'That's because they're lemon trees, dolt.' Erich leaned back in his chair. 'Hey waiter, five beers!'

'Four,' said Peter.

'Excuse me, no beer, Heil Hitler,' stammered the waiter in half-eaten German. 'C'e *vino*. We have wine, a good bottle, from *Vesuvio* grapes . . .'

Erich threw his hands in the air, as if to say, what can you expect in such a backwater? The waiter's face screwed up in concern. Erich rolled his eyes.

'It's all right, we aren't going to shoot you for running a lousy establishment. Coffee will do, *per favore. Molto*

molto coffee. Hell, who knows the Italian for *mountains of food*?' He gave Peter a sideways look. 'Italian's like Latin. Can't you manage the local lingo, Professor?'

Peter gave Erich's chair a gentle push, almost sending him toppling over. Shielding his eyes he scanned the marina. Boats, barbed wire, buildings . . . how could all these things be normal and yet so utterly alien in their own way? This was Italy. *Italy!* Sun bounced off the bay and birds soared where last night's enemy bombers had been. Further out in the harbour water sparkled over the dark, grey hulks of drowned ships.

'Nice view,' said Erich.

'If you don't look too closely.'

'No, you idiot, the *view*. Look!'

There was a girl.

Erich whistled, so did Lanky and Jupp. Heini showed a sudden interest in the cleanliness of his nails. Peter wondered how anyone could look so swish in such a dingy town. She wore a green velvet dress, white socks and shining leather shoes. Her black hair was held back by a sleek satin bow and she had a leather satchel slung across her body. She walked through the dirt like some sort of queen. Trotting a few paces behind her was a wire-haired mongrel dog with absurdly long legs and eyes like bright coal.

Things got a bit jumbled next, when Peter tried to remember how the whole trick started.

Just as the smart girl approached, two stray beggar children emerged from a side street and sidled up to the café. The boy, knee-high to a cricket, had a red *diavolo* puppet with a big grin and perky horns. '*Hallo Hallo buongiorno*,' he said, showing yellow teeth as he grinned. He was all scabs and scars.

The beggar girl didn't speak. She had a mouthful of thumb. As she sucked on it she stroked one dirty finger down the side of an equally dirty nose. She had a headless rag doll tucked under her arm.

Peter's lip curled. How could people let their children sink to this? In a supposedly civilised country too? It just showed the Italians needed Germany on their side, to sort things out.

The smart girl ignored the beggars, just as she'd no doubt ignore a pile of filth in the street.

'*Buongiorno*,' she said.

'*Buongiorno*!' the soldiers chorused in reply. They smiled like wolves. Peter found himself putting his cap straight and sitting up properly.

Erich muttered, 'Told you we'd get lucky. It's the uniforms. Magnets.'

The girl slipped one hand into her satchel and

37

suddenly a rainbow of postcards was spread on the café table followed by an array of gaudy souvenirs.

'Maybe we'll get to see some of these places,' Peter said, eyeing the postcards.

'Bomb sites?' scoffed Erich.

'Ancient ruins. That's a Greek temple. These are Roman houses from Pompeii, you know, the town destroyed by the volcano. This is a house in Herculaneum, right on the seashore, wiped out at the same time. There you are – that's a shot of the cone of Vesuvius. The Romans didn't even know it was a volcano till it erupted all over them. It's only dormant now, not extinct. Actually we're not far from the place where a philosopher, Pliny the Younger, wrote a description of the catastrophe back in AD79 . . . except . . . that's just history.'

Shut up, shut up! he told himself savagely. You're not a kid behind a desk with your hand in the air any more.

He turned to the girl. 'Hey, excuse me, I'll have three postcards and stamps for Germany if you've got them.'

Erich said, 'She doesn't understand.'

Peter held up three fingers.

The girl's smile didn't reach her eyes even though she moved so close she brushed his leg. The others were watching him, expecting him to make a move. Perhaps he should say something. It was only fair to be polite. Speaking slowly he asked, 'What's your name?'

She looked at Erich as she answered in excellent German, 'My name is Vittoria.'

'Nice,' said Peter. 'Like the German word, Viktoria?'

'Like the English Queen Victoria.'

Erich leaned in. 'The English are cowards! We kicked them out of Europe years ago.'

'They'll be back,' she replied. 'Bringing friends with them.'

Peter frowned. 'We're your friends now. Hitler, Mussolini, they're on the same side, remember? We're here to protect you against the enemy.'

'Protect yourselves, paratroopers,' she said, or did he imagine it, because she'd have to be mad to speak to them like that, when they had machine guns propped up against the table and enough muscles between them to move a mountain.

She took payment for the goods and sauntered off, the little dog still a few paces behind. They all watched her go. 'Too young for me anyway,' said Erich, who was all of eighteen. 'What would you say, she's fifteen? Sixteen?'

Minutes passed. Coffee was gulped down. Cigarettes were lit, smoked, stubbed out and flicked to the floor.

Then Lanky patted his pocket in search of a fresh packet.

'Hey! I had a whole wad of cash . . .'

Erich checked his own pockets. Picked.

Heart rolling over, Peter went straight for his most precious thing – his diary. Gone.

The two beggars scampered down the marina as fast as their bare feet could carry them. Erich was fast, Peter faster. He seized the kids. Shook them. Dropped them. Closed his eyes briefly. Waited for Erich to catch up.

'What was it you said about thieves in Naples – they'd fleece you rotten then sell you your own kit back at ten times the price?'

'Something like that,' said Erich. 'Have they got our money?'

'Nothing but clay marbles and tears. The brats are clean.' Suddenly the episode made sense. Peter swore. 'Rats! What about the girl?'

'What about her?'

'Which way did she go?'

'From the café? Some side street . . . after that I don't know. Hey, Peter! Wait!'

Peter was halfway back to the marina when he spotted a tuft of grey hair on legs – the dog that had been with Vittoria. The dog looked at him and seemed to grin. When Peter ran towards it, the dog ran too, into a maze of crooked streets, weaving between stalls drying pasta under dusty awnings, around clogged-up drains, past crones stirring bubbling pots of octopus stew in sunless corners . . .

Peter was dazzled as the narrow alley opened into a little piazza with burnt-orange houses looming over a dry marble fountain. There was the dog again. It crouched in the arch of a great wooden door guarding a coil of fallen ribbon.

The door was shut. He ran up to it. Began beating on it. Almost gave up. Caught his breath. Fell forward as the door opened.

Culture

July 1943

Vittoria clicked the great door shut. She needed a moment, just a moment to catch her breath. Thank heaven for the dim, cool quiet of the house.

That was close!

Too close.

The plan was to *steal* from the soldiers, not openly defy them. Why hadn't she kept her anger hidden? There'd been something about that paratrooper's easy arrogance, thinking he could just strut around her town, doling out small change for pictures of places he'd come to conquer . . .

Stop.

Remember who drove the tanks and carried the guns.

She took a breath, wishing she could simply kneel and press her hot face against the cold marble stairs. Better still, wishing the last few years would peel away and she'd be a little girl again, running upstairs to her mother's arms for a kiss, a smile and a day without war.

The moment passed. Time to be organised again. Nonna would be wondering where she was.

Nonna's kingdom was the kitchen at the back of the vast building. It was a crude vaulted room with a smoke-black ceiling and a table bleached white from ferocious scrubbings. Nonna sat at this table grinding away at a boxy machine. Ages-old, she had skin like walnut shells and hands shaped like ancient olive branches. Her eyes were a pale watery white, edging on almost-blind. When she coughed her very bones shook. She was the only servant left.

'Where have you been, child? The Contessa's ordered fresh coffee for the morning's guests and here's the last of the coffee beans – not much more than dust.'

'They are only Germans. Let them drink acorn powder, like the rest of us have to. I suppose they brought nothing but Berlin newspapers and dirty boots?'

'She was asking for you, your aunt. I said you were fetching fresh breakfast rolls.'

'Nina is sending some from the bakery . . . Holy saints!'

She froze as four hefty knocks echoed through the house. More guests? Or . . . No. It wasn't possible. She'd been too quick, too clever. The police couldn't have tracked her – wouldn't *dare* accuse her!

Bang bang bang! More knocking.

Dear God in heaven with all the angels, let it not be the German military police – those men with faces as hard as volcanic rock and prisons so deep underground rumour said they tunnelled all the way to hell . . .

'Nonna, quick, where can I hide my satchel?' she whispered. 'No, don't answer the door yet, let me just . . . Have you a comb? Oh, there isn't time.'

The front door shook again.

Nonna reached out and caught Vittoria's dress. 'Child, what is happening?'

'Nothing. You can answer the door, just go slowly . . .'

She fled upstairs with the tray of coffee. Straightened her dress. Smoothed her hair. Discovered her hair ribbon was lost. No time to go and find it. No time to spit in the coffee either. Chin up, shoulders back – *a straight back is a strong back*! Deep breath, pleasant smile and . . . in she went, heart racing like a car on a Grand Prix track.

The Contessa's salon was thick with a fug of old alcohol and fresh tobacco smoke. Heavy drapes of lace turned sunshine into a murky beige light, all the better for hiding signs of dereliction ... Pale patches on the walls where valuable paintings had once hung. Gaps in the dust where silverware was once displayed. Odd arrangements of furniture to cover bare patches in the carpet.

Even her aunt looked forlorn, like a fragile sort of flower arranged in a vase without any water. The Contessa Isabella Sanfelice wore a lemon-yellow silk dress that clung to every bone. Vittoria recognised it. One of her mother's.

'Vittoria ... Coffee. Excellent. Let me help pour ...' The Contessa's voice dropped to a murmur. 'Serve the highest ranks first and do not stand near the curtains. We hardly wish anyone to see your frock is made of the same fabric. It looks a little short. Have you been growing? Never mind now. What is that dreadful noise downstairs? I have set some music on the piano. Go and play for us.'

'Beethoven again? To make *them* feel at home?' Vittoria glanced at the German officers clustered on every soft seat.

'Manners! Never forget your position, Vittoria. Your family honour. We must still uphold standards of behaviour even to persons who are not our social equals. Remember we trace our line back to the ancient Roman aristocrats, for all your mother married beneath her. So hush! Play!'

Vittoria felt her chin rise. As a young girl she'd had a piece of holly pinned to the front neckline of her dress – a sharp reminder that a lady could be forced to beg, borrow and steal to survive, but her chin must never droop.

The house echoed with knocks again.

Who was that at the door?

Since the piano was set at one end of the salon, facing the wall, she couldn't view the room directly, but she faced a large speckled mirror etched with Sanfelice heraldry. She saw the reflection of the salon door opening. She nearly fell off the piano stool when she recognised the soldier who entered.

How had he found her, the devil?

He stood to attention. His eyes flickered about the salon. He looked like a boy who'd been brought before the headmaster for a beating. Good. He didn't belong in the salon. None of them did. Why couldn't all the Germans just *go home* and leave Italy alone? Everything had been wonderful before the war and now . . .

'You can't just leave me here with Aunt Isabella!' she'd objected, when her parents said they had to leave.

46

Papa's newspaper was sending him to Rome, where the big stories were.

'It'll be safer in Naples,' they said.

She said, 'Then you should stay here with me! At least Mama could!'

'We'll send a letter every day,' they said. 'The Germans will leave soon enough. The war can't last for ever.'

Naples wasn't safe. There had been no letters for weeks. The Germans were everywhere. The war was dragging on.

In the mirror she watched a bulky major struggle to rise from his armchair. He patted his face with a silk handkerchief and bawled at the young soldier.

'What in God's name do you mean, hammering on the door of a respectable household at this hour? I want name, regiment and commanding officer!'

The boy's answers shot out like bullets.

Private Peter Schäfer, Private Adolf Hitler, at that moment Vittoria despised all soldiers equally.

The Contessa said, '*Guten Morgen*, Peter Schäfer. Why are you creating such a fuss at my door?' She spoke German with a lazy Italian accent, unlike Vittoria, who had learned the language from a more exacting governess.

'*Entschuldigen*,' the boy said. 'I'm sorry. I was chasing a thief.'

'Oh? What sort of thief?'

Mirror eyes met and Vittoria held Peter's gaze. Slowly but surely she drew a line across her throat – what she would do with a knife if he betrayed her. His face hardened. Why should he feel threatened? He had a machine gun capable of firing hundreds of rounds a minute. Even so, he paused.

'It was . . . a local, ma'am.'

'And what did this thief take that was so precious?'

'She . . . A book, ma'am.'

'Some filth, I expect!' spluttered the overstuffed major. 'Soldiers today just aren't made of the right stuff any more.'

A more refined officer looked up from his newspaper. Vittoria recognised him as new to the salon that week, a snobbish sort who fancied himself cultured because he spoke a little Italian. His name was Julius Schlegel and he had lieutenant-colonel stripes.

'Was it trash?' he asked the boy.

Peter shook his head. 'No, sir. It was a selection of . . . of Latin authors, sir. An old school book. I . . . I write in it as a diary, sir.'

Liar! Vittoria didn't see how a boy like him could be educated. Soldiers didn't learn Latin. She began to coax music from the old piano, softly, softly, so she could still listen in. She saw Schlegel lean forward and hoped he'd catch the boy out.

'Unusual reading for a paratrooper. Even our officers aren't always so discerning. The book includes all the war commentaries, I suppose? Josephus, Caesar, Marcus Aurelius . . . ?'

'Horace's *Epistles* too, sir, and some passages from Virgil – the *Aeneid* and the *Eclogues*.'

Schlegel beamed. 'Excellent! I daresay you'd prefer some of the more vulgar poems by Catullus and Ovid?'

'Possibly, sir.'

'Filth!' spouted the major again.

'Yes, sir.'

Schlegel lit a new cigarette. 'By coincidence I too have been immersed in the classics since arriving in Italy. Our Italian friends . . .' – a sweep of the cigarette included the Contessa and Vittoria – '. . . they are remarkably lax about their national treasures. I mean the archaeology salvaged from the skirts of Vesuvius – from Pompeii and Herculaneum in particular, the Roman towns destroyed by the eruption in AD79.'

Vittoria felt a sudden chill and paused in her playing. Schlegel's voice deepened.

'Buried at the moment of a dark and hideous death, covered with ash and volcanic mud, lying side by side with the bodies of those who once cherished and used them, after nearly two thousand years of silence these artefacts have been brought into the light again. Pots with food still in them. Rings still on the fingers of skeletons. Artworks. Silver. Gold! All the treasures of antiquity. Germany has no desire to see these unique items destroyed by enemy bombs or looted by enemy thieves. It is my intention to have these artefacts taken away for safe-keeping.'

'I suppose our Roman treasures will look impressive in your Berlin Museum, safe from *other* criminals?'

She hadn't meant to speak – the words just erupted from her mouth. Schlegel bent his head towards her in a mock bow.

'Forgive me, Fraülein Sanfelice, the treasures will not go to Berlin, with the exception of one or two pieces selected personally by Hitler's closest colleagues – keen collectors, you understand. No, the remainder are to stay here in Italy, in a mountain-top fortress north-east of Naples. Perhaps you know of it – the monastery of Monte Cassino?'

How dare he call her *Fraülein*, as if she was actually German! She was a *signorina*. Italian!

'My name is not Sanfelice, it is Vittoria Venafro, after my father, Vittorio Venafro. He writes for—'

'Hush, child!' said the Contessa quickly. 'If you won't play music, at least pour some more coffee for our guests. Pay no attention to my niece, gentlemen! She misses her mother, it is only natural. They are absent, her parents. The war! And you, boy, there is no thief here, except time, which makes these happy hours all too short. Nonna will show you out. *Auf Wiedersehen*. Go, go!'

Yes, go, thought Vittoria. *Get out, all of you. Out of my house, out of my country, no don't look at me, Peter rotten Schäfer! I'm not giving you your book back! Go*!

The major patted her cheek when she poured him fresh coffee. In her mind she shot him dead and won a medal for the deed. Let her father write about *that* on the front page of the morning paper!

In reality she calmly played another movement of Beethoven. When the last note was sounded she closed the piano lid, curtseyed to her aunt and left the salon. Not long afterwards the major began to fidget and fuss, patting pockets and harrumphing grumpily.

'Has anyone seen my lighter? I swear I had it earlier. It's silver, etched with the *Reich* eagle . . .'

She sold it the next morning, gave more money to Nonna for food, and some to Doll and Diavolo in return for their diversion at the café. That was their usual arrangement for 'work'.

51

The paratrooper's book was just a school text, as he'd said, with pencil scrawls in the margins, some pathetic letters – why should *he* receive them when she never did? – and a few photographs of smug, fat-faced Germans, including one pretty girl who'd obviously paid for a studio shot, otherwise no one could look that flawless.

Worthless. Just like its previous owner.

Clueless

Dr Shepherd stirred a third spoon of sugar into her tea and smiled.

'The girl Peter met was a thief. A little aristocrat fallen on hard times, having to wear clothes cut from the curtains. War can be a great leveller in society. Her name was Vittoria Venafro. She robbed soldiers who were new to Naples, including Peter and his friends. Mostly in Naples it was boys who ran wild during the war. The girls, well, they had to be more careful, especially the pretty ones, you can imagine why. The gangs of boys were known as *scugnizzi*. Vittoria Venafro, how do you say, *disdained* them. She thought she would show them that a girl could do what they did. The tricks those little criminals tried! One was to have a diversion, perhaps a barrel suddenly toppled, or beggars asking for money, then the theft would take place. Or, imagine this: Craig, I am passing you in the street and I steal your watch. Quickly I pass it to Denise, who vanishes . . .'

'By magic?'

'Into another street. Now I turn to Craig and say, "Sir, I think you have been robbed," and Craig shouts for the *carabinieri*, the police, and they may search me . . .'

'But Denise has got the loot all along.'

'Exactly. Now Vittoria was not *advantaged*, do you say? She had learned how to be a lady, not a *ladrone*, a robber. But she had talent! Queen of Thieves, they called her in the end.'

Queen of Thieves? That sounded like the sort of career path Mum might not endorse, though it was probably more glamorous than my current job option of Having No Idea. It also raised several questions, like, why wasn't this Vittoria arrested? Why wasn't she in school? Didn't the Germans *shoot* just about everyone who even looked the wrong way, let alone actually broke a law?

I tried these teasers out on the old lady.

'Oh yes, the punishment for looting could be death. Soldiers were clever too. They knew *scugnizzi* climbed on to the back of trucks, even when they were driving along roads. There would be a man hiding in the back of the truck with a knife. He was ready to *slice* the fingers.'

'Just cos kids were hitching a lift?' Craig asked.

I said, 'Dummy – cos they were nicking stuff from the back of the truck.'

'But then they'd have no fingers!'

'Serves them right. Where were you when they were handing morals out?' Which was all evading other questions I wanted answering: 'Did this Peter get his money back? Was Vittoria shot?'

Dr Shepherd really stretched the suspense by taking a long gulp of tea.

'Vittoria did not steal Peter's money. She took something far more precious. A book. His diary, you see. They made him a soldier but he could not forget his school, not so quickly.'

That joggled my brain cells a bit. *Something was taken . . . Something was taken, it must be returned . . .*

'So did Peter get his book back?'

'Not immediately. There was a war in between, and other things. Stranger things . . .'

Oh no you don't, I thought. Out with it, you old bat! What?!

But she mumbled some rubbish about *troubled spirits* and then I heard Mum's car pull up outside – the perfect excuse to escape.

'Wait a minute,' said Craig, just as we were almost Scot-free. 'I really have lost my watch.'

'No, no,' said Dr Shepherd. 'I have it here . . .'

And there it was, magicked from somewhere and handed back. That little trick won Craig's undying respect. I was still uneasy.

Troubled spirits.

So the old lady wanted to be mysterious, did she? Dealing out snippets to see if we'd be hooked? Well we weren't. At least, I wasn't. I got enough war on the TV and enough history at school, without breaking my heart over some boy soldier from a squillion years ago. Craig wouldn't stop gabbing on about it though, paratroopers this and paratroopers that, till I threatened to smack him one.

'What's brought all this on?' Mum asked him, after the millionth factoid about the bloody paras.

'I went next door to see Winnie.'

'I don't want you bothering the neighbours.'

'It's not bothering. She likes having her tummy tickled and I feed her biscuits.'

Mum looked alarmed. I quickly explained that Winnie was next door's dog. Mum sighed. 'Please tell me Mrs Shepherd hasn't offered to break into the house again! Nice though it was of her to look after you and get the door mended, I wish—'

'It's *Doctor* Shepherd, not Mrs.'

That set Mum off on a rant about all the doctors in the world, who were apparently arrogant condescending pigs. She gets like that when there's been a stinky shift at the hospital, because she's a nurse. Always overworked and knackered. There was no point saying, not *that* kind of doctor. She went all melodramatic.

'Both of you promise me you won't ever work in a hospital, unless you're one of the doctors, of course.'

She only took up nursing so she could get a job whenever Dad moved from one army base to another. She was stuck working at a hospital when Dad got sent abroad for a six-month tour in the Gulf.

Craig took up his imaginary machine gun and started spraying bullets round the kitchen. 'No problemo – I'm gonna be a paratrooper. Mum, did you know the Germans had paras in the Second World War? Some of them were just boys. More young than Rich.'

'*Younger*,' I said.

Mum asked if Rich had called, or if there were any letters.

Nope.

Craig just doesn't know when to stop. 'But some of the paras were only fifteen, Mum, same as Denise.'

She said, 'I expect Hitler had to start cradle-robbing,

57

given how many armies he was getting through.'

We had pizza for tea and I watched a movie with Mum, a romance about skinny girls getting married in big dresses. I said I had homework but actually I went upstairs to write to Rich, on one of the *blueys* we get free from the Post Office. Rich gets them free too only he doesn't write so often. He says real letters are nicer than emails.

Hello, how are you? We're fine apart from Craig who's mad, obviously, but you already knew that. I'm fabulosus. School's boring. Mum's sending you some more loo roll – lucky you. Craig spilled the fish but they didn't die. Are you all right? Do kids in Afghanistan ever nick kit off you? Not much news here. Have you heard about German paratroopers in World War 2? Not long till Christmas. Are you coming home? Hope you're OK, Luv u. Denise.

Kiss or no kiss?
Kiss.

X

Too bad I posted it before Craig's latest adventure, else

there would have been more to report on the Loo Roll front. Here's how it went:

Craig's coming home from school just minding his own business when he sees this van on our street, the sort with a cab and an open back. He starts thinking about street kids in Naples. He thinks, no way could you jump on the back of a moving truck.

Any normal person might've left it there, but no, young Mr Cooper esquire suddenly decides to see if it can be done, so he drops his backpack and leaps on the truck with his arm on the tailboard and his legs all bendy so they don't drag on the road. So far so good. Except he'd reckoned without one tiny detail. The small fact that the tailboard wasn't properly fastened.

Now we get the slo-mo tipping open of the tailboard and the comedy tipping over of the boy. He landed on his bum and was promptly bombed by boxes.

If only I'd been there to see it. There was a bona fide eyewitness, Craig said. An old bloke (too old to have a mobile to video it and post it on the internet). This bloke got out of the back of a taxi and stood staring at Craig – laughing at him. Worse, the bloke started picking up boxes and piling them on the kerb – actually helping him out. The van driver came back later, when he realised half his stuff had mysteriously fallen out. I got home in time to see Craig scraping his bag off the road ... and said-old-bloke hefting a large black case up the path to number sixty-four ... obviously he was Dr Shepherd's husband.

'What'd he say?' I asked.

Craig mumbled, 'Something about if we ran low again we could call round and they'd spare a roll.'

You see, the best bit is, my angelic little brother had accidentally robbed the van of a million boxes of LOO PAPER! Classic.

Then – funny how it happens – the Shepherds lived next door to us for eons without us meeting and next thing I know, Dr Shepherd barged into me at the corner shop. We stood by the big fridges, which were humming really loudly. She just pointed at my basket and said, 'You are eating only this for dinner tonight?' No hello or anything.

'Fish fingers are good for you,' I said. 'They've got omega three.' (Or is it six? Can't remember.)

She said she liked fish. Looked at her watch. Muttered, 'Never enough time. Not long until August twenty-fourth. Not long at all. You must ... No. First I'll show you something else. *Tesoro*. Treasure. You'll come and see treasure, yes?'

Not long till August? It was only pigging *October*!

August was a million years away! I let her put a bag of apples in my basket – no harm done if I took them straight out when she wasn't looking. Then I couldn't help myself. I had to know.

'What sort of treasure?'

Herculaneum

August 1943

Vittoria hoped to sneak past the kitchen without Nonna noticing. Her little dog had other ideas.

'Get down off my dress!' she hissed. 'I'll crucify you if there are claw marks! Down! No, wait, what's that on your fur? Just fluff? Ugh! You're infested again. No wonder your name is Nit. I should never have rescued you from those horrible boys throwing stones at you for grenade practice.'

Nit's tail wagged merrily.

'No! Don't bark! I don't want the whole world to know we're off on a treasure hunt.'

Too late.

'Is that you, child?'

'I'm going out, Nonna.'

Nonna was at the kitchen doorway, leaning on the cold stone wall. 'Out? Where, out?'

'Fishing. Don't tell my aunt, she wouldn't like it.'

'There are no fish! That dog! In the house again! It is shameful.' Nit barked. Nonna tossed him a piece of cheese rind and laughed. 'The Contessa, she asks, *Nonna, have you seen my tan leather gloves? Nonna, where is my silk slipper*, and that creature, I know, takes them under my bed to chew. Perhaps we'll be eating shoes before long. Boiling up leather belts . . .'

'I'm getting food today, Nonna, I promise.'

'If your mother could see you! Come back before nightfall, child. It's not a day for wandering in the dark. Yes, look at me like an old mad woman, but it is not superstition, it is true, and has been for centuries. Do you know what the date is?'

'The twenty-third, no, twenty-fourth.'

'The twenty-fourth of August. The day when the boundary between living and dead is broken. As truly as I stand before you now the dead walk, may the holy Mother of God protect us all.'

Nonna kissed the cross on her rosary. Vittoria just shook her head and set some money on the kitchen table. Opening the front door she stumbled over two

63

tiny children who'd been curled up together like stray cats. Once she'd asked them their names, but they'd been orphans so long they couldn't remember, so she named them after the toys they carried everywhere – Doll and Diavolo.

'Tell me you didn't spend the night in our doorway! What about the place I showed you at the back of Nina's bakery?'

Diavolo patted Nit's wiry fur. 'Nina was nice but Mr Dragone put rat poison down and said it was for us and chased us out.'

'Try San Pietro – Father Tomaso will find you somewhere in the church.'

'He smells. We're ready to work. Behold – I have my puppet and my sister will dance . . .'

'We're not working today. I'm busy.'

'We'll help you.'

Help? Wouldn't that be nice?

Vittoria sighed. 'When did you two last eat? Oh never mind, come with me. It's a bit of a walk but I've got an idea where we might find some seafood.'

'There are guns on the marina,' said Diavolo. 'They shoot anyone who takes a boat out – even those fishermen who used an old door for a raft.'

'It'll be fine where we're going. Keep up.'

Doll unsucked her thumb to speak. 'Is Anna-Maria coming too?'

'Anna-Maria will turn up, I'm sure.'

'And Nit is coming?'

'Leading the way.'

'And Nina too?'

'Nina's the only one actually invited. Come on.'

God in heaven with all the angels playing harps! Was she some sort of Pied Piper that other children attached themselves to her like nits to a dog? There was Doll, Diavolo, then Anna-Maria and her cousin Tonio appearing from nowhere ... Poor Anna-Maria! Mute since her parents were killed in a bombing raid, but legs like a colt. Perfect for grab-and-run tactics. Nina was different, of course. Nina was a friend. She also hid stolen goods at the Dragoné family bakery because the Contessa was apt to prowl round *Casa Sanfelice* looking for things to sell.

It was good to see Nina waiting in the Piazza Mercata with sun shining on her blonde hair, waving, smiling and flourishing a long loaf of bread.

She said, 'I didn't know you'd have company. I only brought enough for two.'

'They follow me everywhere,' Vittoria whispered, glancing at the huddle of children in her shadow. 'Why won't they go away?'

'You're the Queen. We're just loyal subjects.'

'I don't feel like being Queen today.'

'Then tell them to go home.'

'What home? Well, perhaps there's safety in numbers. We're going to Resina.'

'What's in Resina?'

'It's not what's in Resina, but what's *under* it . . . Two-thousand-year-old treasure if we're lucky, in the old Roman ruins of Herculaneum. A German officer was talking about it in the Contessa's salon.'

'Treasure?' Nina's eyes lit up. 'Enough to get food? To leave the bakery? Papa had me up all night on firewatch and he was boiling mad this morning. Looters tried to break into the flour store again but I'd fallen asleep and didn't realise. If we found treasure you could buy a palace and have a proper throne and I'd never work again . . .'

Vittoria laughed. 'I don't want a palace or thrones. I want an enormous cake, oozing with fresh cream, surrounded by the world's biggest strawberries.'

And I want my mama and papa home and nothing to do all day but have them look after me and tell me they'll never go away again . . .

'Can I have cake?' asked Doll.

'I want ice cream,' said Diavolo. 'A whole bowl all to myself.'

'If we find treasure you can swim in ice cream,' Vittoria promised. 'First there's a seven-mile walk south round the bay.'

Seven miles! Diavolo wanted to know why the soldiers couldn't give them a lift. 'All the army trucks are going the same way as us and we could steal a gun.'

'Try it and see how soon you get shot,' said Vittoria.

Nina said, 'The Germans are so serious these days, look at them. Papa reckons the war's going badly for them. Maybe they'll all go home.'

Vittoria watched as truck after truck rumbled past, each full of blank-faced soldiers or weapons, or God only knew what. She didn't spot Peter Schäfer, or that friend of his with hair like a squirrel.

'Germany's thousands of miles north. The trucks and tanks are going south.'

'Then they're afraid the Allies might invade. Papa says the Americans would make big orders for fresh white bread and pay in dollars, and the English drink tea at four o'clock and get sunburnt. Do you think that's where all these troops are going, to stop an invasion?'

'They can be going full speed to hell, for all I care. I'm sick of soldiers, all of them.'

Resina was dry and dirty. She led her minions through the modern town. It was hard to keep looking resolute and optimistic when the site of the treasure – the ancient town of Herculaneum – no longer looked anything like a fabulous seaside resort for rich Romans. Roofless walls reached up to the sun. Glassless windows stared out on to empty streets. The ruins were full of weeds and dry cat droppings. That snooty officer in the salon, Schlegel, he must have been lying when he said there was still treasure to find. Only a bulldozer could dig through all that rock-hard volcanic debris.

Suddenly she shivered and turned to see who was staring at her.

No one.

Apart from her dusty band of children the noon-hot streets were deserted. So why did she feel cold? She looked beyond the town. Rising above the sad buildings was the great mass of Vesuvius. A lazy breath of steam curled from its grey summit.

She jumped. Diavolo was tugging her skirt.

'I'm hungry,' he whined. 'So's my sister.'

'You'd rather fill your bottomless pit of a tummy than look for buried treasure?'

All the children nodded.

'Fine. We'll have to get past that barbed wire first, to

get on to the beach. Anna-Maria, Tonio, tear off that sign saying *Danger* and squash the wire with it. If we're lucky we'll get snails, winkles and limpets. Ignore the battleships, they're only after the Allies.'

'What if there's mines?' murmured Nina.

'I don't want to be exploded,' little Tonio suddenly wailed.

'There won't be any mines,' said Vittoria loudly.

No mines, no snails, no winkles. No fish either. Not a single nibble on the strings they dangled into the sea. That left limpets, which had to be bashed off the rocks with pointed stones. Nit went rat hunting. The children didn't have the energy to join in.

Nina said, 'Let's make a fire.'

'Nothing to burn,' said Vittoria.

'What about that book you stole?'

'I'm reading it.'

It was true. Late at night Vittoria would creep from bed and pull aside the blackout curtains, turning the pages towards the moonlight to read Peter Schäfer's ambling German words. One by one she studied the photographs tucked in between the pages. The woman with the cheap fur tippet and the cascading chins – that had to be his mother. The tired-looking man standing next to a tractor – that would be the father. There was a sister too – a round little cherub with yellow curls. There was another picture of two boys in uniform, with *Me & Erich!* scribbled on the back. They were handsome murdering devils, she'd give them that.

The rest of the book was in Latin, and therefore useless. There on the beach she tore a few pages out to make paper cones for the limpets, which were gouged out of their shells to be eaten raw. Even though her stomach was twisting itself into knots she said she wasn't hungry and gave her share away.

'Don't wipe your fingers on your clothes,' she told the children. They used their bare skin instead.

When the sun got too high and hot she watched as the others curled into cavities in the rocks and warmed themselves like stray dogs. She stayed on watch at the sea edge. She was itching to be digging for treasure at Herculaneum but the sparkling blue of the bay made her brain dance. Her body swayed like the sea and her mind seemed to slip sideways.

What happened to the hours? Did she doze off? The sun was gone and the stars were out. Once again there was a chilly edge to the air – peculiar for August. The other children were still deeply asleep. She wished she had blankets or something, to cover them. How was she going to keep them all warm and fed when winter began to bite? It was hard being Queen. She screwed her eyes up to focus on a star and wished, fiercely, that there was someone who'd come and take care of *her* for a change.

A breeze blew down the volcano's slopes and out to sea.

She didn't hear or directly see the man approach, just became aware of his awkward gait. He sat down on a rock some way off and stared across the sea as if waiting for something to appear. Eventually he tipped his head back. He pointed at the sky. His words weren't Italian but they prickled like something familiar. He pointed again and repeated himself.

The stars are beautiful.

The moon had risen, a big white disc. Bomber's Moon, they called it when it was full, or only slightly nibbled at one edge. It was well named. Almost every night the Allies came to sprinkle explosives, sometimes American bombs, sometimes British. Even as she sat on the sea edge she heard the distant drone of approaching aircraft. Soon there'd be fireworks lighting the sky and smoke on the night horizon. Doll and Diavolo whimpered in their sleep.

'Don't worry,' she always told them. 'It's only God moving furniture about.'

Now she was worried about a closer danger. She felt around for a rock weapon. Something about the stranger felt very wrong, even though he hadn't yet offered to rape, rob or break her. What use was Nit as a guard dog? The little scruff was sleeping with the other children, splayed across them in happy exhaustion.

The man limped closer to sea until his leather boots were almost in the water. He looked out across the bay but his words blew back towards her.

Once the waves came right to the town ... when there was a town.

She stared at him.

He seemed to speak again. *Greetings. What is your name?*

'None of your business.'

I am Justinius. Gaius Justinius Aquila.

When he turned his head to look at her she saw he had an almost ugly face with a big, long nose. There was a bag of tools slung across his back. His legs were bare and he had a strange loose top that came to his knees. What was that hanging from his belt? A scabbard?

'Are you a soldier?'

I was.

He wasn't German or Italian, she knew that much. Could he be English or American? A spy? She tried to swallow her fear. God in heaven with all the angels playing harps and wearing halos – what sort of soldier had a *sword*?

She raised her chin and squared her shoulders. 'My name is Vittoria Venafro.'

Well met, Vittoria. You are young to be alone. Where is your mother?

'Rome. Papa too. They're coming to get me soon.'

What are you doing here?

'Getting food.'

Those children, are they hungry?

'Starving more like! Haven't you noticed the war?'

There is always a war. After this one, there 'll be another and another.

'Then people should learn not to have any more.'

People do . . . but only the ones who suffer the wars, not the ones who make them. These children, they are your family?

'Hardly. One's a friend, I can't shake the rest off. They're orphans.'

You can't save them. In the end they will all die screaming. You'll try to save yourself and leave them behind.

'What sort of talk is that?' Vittoria answered scornfully. 'I'll look after them.'

And who looks after you?

'I do!'

You will die too. The war is bigger than you are.

'I defy the war! The world! The stupid volcano – all of it!' She stood up on the rocks with Vesuvius as her backdrop and the moon as her spotlight.

The man took a silent step towards her. He fixed her with unblinking grey eyes.

So you believe help will come even at the end of hope?

'No, I don't. I think I'll manage anyway, without anyone's help.'

That made him smile. She turned away and whistled to Nit, but when the little dog finally trotted over she saw the man had gone. Nit nosed in the shadows. Warily, Vittoria approached. The man had dropped something as he left. Something small and dark, made of leather.

'Give it to me, no, you can't eat it.'

She prised it out of the dog's mouth. It was a leather purse. Empty? No. When she unknotted the drawstring and opened the purse she saw five bold gold coins twinkling in the moonlight.

Treasure!

Restless Spirits

Craig claimed he'd starved to death twice in the time it took me to go the corner shop and back again that time.

I snapped, 'Next time *you* buy dinner. I do everything round here.'

'Mum says you have to look after me. Not fish fingers again!'

'Since when did you care?'

'I'm building up my athletic physique.'

Athletic. Physique. Two words I didn't even know Craig could pronounce, let alone apply to himself. Turns out he was taking all this paratroop stuff a bit too much to heart.

He said, 'Dr Shepherd's told me the tenth commandment of the *Fallschirmjäger*. Hang on, I wrote it down somewhere, here it is: "Keep your eyes wide open. Tune yourself to the topmost pitch. Be nimble as a greyhound, as tough as leather, as hard as Krupp steel and so you shall be the German warrior incarnate." '

'Wow. And?'

'And I've joined the cross country team at school, first meeting tomorrow. D'you know where my trainers are?'

'The ones you left out in the garden sometime over the summer holiday?'

He said rude things and went out, leaving me in peace to grill the fish fingers and put chips in the oven. I was in a bit of a daze really. Dr Shepherd hadn't said *much* on the way home from the shop, just enough to drive me crazy. Forget finding out about treasure. She'd wanted to know whether I believed in *ghosts*. (This from a woman who was wearing wellies printed with bumble bees and ladybirds.)

She said that according to the old Roman calendar there was a day when the boundaries between the underworld of Hades and the land of the living were dissolved. On this day the dead walked freely, like Hallowe'en, she said.

I wasn't going to swallow it whole.

'Hallowe'en's just people dressed up pretending. No one believes there are real witches around.'

'Not witches, *ghosts*. Shadows. Shades. Restless spirits. You do not believe in possibilities? Your mind is closed?'

'No! But ghosts are just a superstition.'

'Perhaps. Strange things are called superstition before science advances enough to explain them. Many Romans believed in ghosts. Sensible, intelligent people. Their towns had a special line ploughed round called a *pomerium*. How would you call it? A magical border which stopped the dead coming into the town. Nowadays, cemeteries are among the streets and houses of the living, but for the Romans all tombs and graves had to be beyond the *pomerium*, outside the town, in the *necropolis*. The city of the dead.'

'That's a bit grisly.'

'One festival of the dead was on August twenty-fourth. Did you know it is the same day Vesuvius erupted in Anno Domini 79? It was the worst of all the eruptions. Ash, pumice, they were destructive, but it was poison gas that killed most, in agony. Pompeii and Herculaneum were buried. Thousands ran. Some to the fields, some to the beach at Herculaneum. Uncounted hundreds died. They say the air was as black as Hades, that the sand on the beach turned to glass, that the sea boiled. They say Vesuvius was the mouth of hell itself . . .'

It started to rain on Willow Garth – not ash but water.

'Isn't there usually some scientific explanation for seeing ghosts, you know, like, atmospheric disturbances or jiggling on the optical nerves? There was a thing on telly about it.'

'Yes, yes, I agree.'

'You do?'

'Of course! There are several possible causes for hallucinations of this kind. Cataclysms make people upset, it is well known. Earthquakes before the eruption gave people hallucinations, the Romans recorded this. They did not understand the warning – that the mountain was waking up. Also hunger, sleep deprivation, certain illnesses, all these cause the mind to be confused. It is a terrible thing to be confused. Terrible.'

Oh well, that's that sorted, I thought.

Wrong again.

She stopped at the path to our house and clutched my sleeve, just like the first time we met.

'But do you believe in ghosts, Denise Cooper? Do you believe in the restless dead?'

Her grip was tight. She scared me. I practically ran up the path to my house. *Ghosts*? What's to believe in? When people are dead they're gone. They don't write you letters or remember your birthdays or come to see you in school concerts. I should know. I have a dead dad.

Like I said, the conversation was pointless. Nothing about treasure.

Dinner turned to charcoal. I turned the fire alarm off and opened the back door to let smoke waft out. Over at number sixty-four I could see Dr Shepherd washing up. She grinned and waved as if she was a normal person, not a nutcase.

Craig came squelching out of the garden with a very drippy pair of trainers. He gave the old lady a big thumbs up. I said if he was on a health kick he could make a start on the big bag of apples I'd accidentally bought. Then the phone rang and it was RICHARD!

'When are you coming home?' I asked.

Rich laughed. 'I only just got here!'

'Is there a lot of fighting?'

'Nothing we can't handle. Don't worry about it. We're just on patrol, that sort of thing. Is Craig there?'

Of course Craig was there. He was jumping up and down for the phone like the daft dog next door. Him and Rich always got on better – must be a boy thing. Craig's set on joining the Army Cadets as soon as he hits thirteen. Me, I had a stint, just long enough to prove I was useless at all that military stuff. Can't march, can't shoot, can't see the point in saluting.

Rich couldn't talk for long – all the soldiers share a satellite phone I think – so then I was stuck with Craig blathering on about paras-this and paras-that till I snapped and said I was fed up hearing about war.

Craig deflated. 'You're just saying that cos you're jealous it's us who win the medals.'

'Us?'

'Men. Girls never do anything good. They can't even play football.'

'Men can't have babies!'

'You can't either. I mean, you'd better not, or Mum'll go ballistic.'

'As if I would.'

So next day I had an apple for breakfast, thought *what the hell* and stepped up to join football practice during PE. Craig was wrong about girls and footy – the other players were really good. If they didn't win the ball by skill they had sharp elbows to get me out of the way. I fumbled the ball every time. Got it thumped in my gut, under both feet, anywhere except in the enemy's goal.

Samantha Green's the Under-16s' top striker. At the end of training she cornered me in the changing rooms and said, 'Don't bother coming again, Cooper, you just can't hack it.' She had a bubble of spit in the corner of her mouth. I couldn't help staring at it as she insulted me. She didn't stop there, either, not once her mates had gathered round to give support.

'How's your big brother?' she leered. 'I heard he's a

brave war hero now, or should we call him a war *criminal*? Richard Cooper, the Baby-killing Butcher of Basra!'

What??

I stared at her. 'He's not even in Basra. That's Iraq. Wrong country.'

My voice started cracking and I knew my face was red. I just had to grab my bag and leg it.

Baby killer? Butcher? She was there last summer, wasn't she, when Rich got the boom box out and climbed on top of the bus shelter outside school, to surf to the sound of the Beach Boys? She'd joined in, hadn't she, when he did that charity custard-pie-throwing thing at school and raised over three hundred quid? She even had a crush on him once, I remember, and used to go bombing round town in his rusty red Ford Fiesta. What the hell was she on about now – *war criminal*? He was my *brother*.

Please God, I prayed, tell me that's not Gavin Parker coming down the corridor. Except it was, and he could see I was about to cry.

'You OK, Coop?' he asked.

Oh for a whopping killer machine gun I could fire at the whole world! Oh for one of those hand grenade things I could lob into the girls' changing rooms to obliterate the entire cackling footy team.

'DO I LOOK OK?' I yelled at Gavin before stomping off.

I made new additions to the list of macho things I can't hack:

1) Football *Brand new entry in the number one spot!*
2) Shooting guns
3) Peeing standing up
4) Pretending not to have emotions.

I went to watch the cross-country lot instead. Good thing Craig didn't hear Samantha sounding off about war criminals, he'd've gone ape. He says soldiers have to follow orders else the army can't work, or it starts thinking it's more powerful than a government. Pretty profound stuff coming from a boy who probably can't even spell *military dictatorship*. He's only paraphrasing Dr Know-it-All next door.

Craig's best mate Tariq was watching cross-country too. Normally I give Tariq a mile-wide exclusion zone because he's got this crush-thing on me. That day I didn't see him till too late. Fortunately one of the symptoms of his crush is he can't actually speak to me directly.

The sporty-types were doing laps of the hockey pitch as a warm-up. Craig looked titchy on the start line. Did he realise his shorts were on back-to-front? He set off at a semi-sprint and kept level with the leaders until reality kicked in: he was obviously going to die if he kept running so fast. He slowed to a walk soon enough and had to limp the remaining laps.

At the end Tariq went over to him. 'You're lying in a puddle, mate. Looks like you missed selection for the Olympics.'

I said, 'He finished, didn't he? He'll get good with training. Anyway, like that Roman guy said, *Fortune favours the bold.*'

Craig actually perked up at that. He wasn't ready to smile but he did get up off the grass and he even offered to clean his own filthy kit when we got home. It would've been better if he'd closed the washing machine door properly, but at least the floodwater soaped away all his muddy footprints on the kitchen floor.

Tariq came home with us and we defrosted one of Mum's home-made pizzas from the fridge, loading it with extra cheese. She was back a bit later, carrying a very welcome tub of chocolate ice cream as a treat. Apples just couldn't compete.

She said, 'Didn't you notice this letter pushed through the letterbox?'

'Is it from Rich?'

'I don't think so. It's for you two, look, it says: *Craig and Denise.*'

(I hate it when people put his name first. Don't they

know I'm oldest? Well, middle oldest if you count Rich.)

She handed me a crumpled white envelope and went off to chat with Tariq. There was no stamp on the envelope, so it couldn't be from Rich. No note inside either, just a single coin. A dazzlingly bright gold coin.

Craig bit it.

'Don't eat it, you idiot!'

'I'm checking if it's real.'

'How can you tell by biting it?'

'Dunno, they just do it in films and that.'

I laughed at him and snatched it back. 'It's got to be fake. I bet it's from Mrs Mad Baggage next door. She was going on about treasure before.'

'Whose head's that?'

'Some bloke with a porky face.' We both squinted at the writing over the portrait on one side of the coin. 'Does that say *Vespasian*? Was he an emperor? I've heard of Julius Caesar, and Nero.'

Craig nodded. 'Didn't Nero fiddle taxes or something?'

'*Played* the fiddle. While Rome burned.'

God knows where that bit of useless knowledge came from.

I put Vespasian's coin under my pillow that night. When I finally got to sleep I dreamed of ghosts marching under ripped red flags, of a sky that rained ash and a great grey mountain spitting out fire.

Dogfight

September 1943

Peter couldn't decide which was worse, missing out on a chance to catch the sun or having dust stick to his sweaty skin if he took his shirt off.

Did this country never see rain? The coast road was so dry the mud just blew up in a gritty cloud as the convoy of trucks and tank-destroyers churned up more ruts. Someone should tell the driver he could try going round the massive potholes, instead of straight into them.

Sick of being banged against the hard seat of the open-topped truck he stood up and stretched his legs. Vesuvius drew his gaze at once. Always it was there, watching. So still. So peaceful. Would the road go past the Roman ruins? Would he actually be able to catch a glimpse of Pompeii or Herculaneum?

Erich yawned. 'Get your elbow out of my face, Turnip, and sit down. The view's just the same as it has always been. Seen one earthly paradise, seen them all, that's what I say.'

Paradise? Hadn't they spent the past six weeks embedding tank traps amongst groves of sweet-smelling flowers and setting concrete gun emplacements at every lovely viewpoint? What of the orchards sown with mines among the rotting windfalls, or the sunny meadows strung with explosive wires? Every defensive point was fortified now. Good. Let the Allies try and invade and see how much of a paradise the countryside was!

Boom! Boom! Boom! The air vibrated with a deep booming rhythm. Heavy artillery. The sea was grey with warship steel. If the war was getting closer why was the convoy taking them further away? They were going north now, back towards Naples, while the war was happening in the south, towards the bay of Salerno.

He told Erich he was itching to go and give the Allies a warm welcome.

'You're itching because of the fleas,' said Erich.

Corporal Mahler growled, 'Don't be in such a rush to get killed. We'll get our share.'

Jupp Weiss looked up from a poker game he'd been

running since the convoy set off. 'Makes me want to be sick, he said.

'Not again!' yelled Lanky, who'd nearly been spattered last time Jupp heaved his stomach contents over the side of the truck. 'Hey, don't lob things at me!'

'I meant it makes me sick doing all this grunt work when we could be getting real action. I'm with Turnip on that.'

'Hear hear!' cried Erich. 'Anyone would think we were retreating. I'd spit if I wasn't so thirsty – who's got a drink?'

Peter grinned at the banter. It was great to feel part of things. The locals didn't seem to be enjoying themselves so much. The convoy rumbled through one sad village after another. Why didn't the Italian children wave or salute any more? He reached for a ration pack thinking to throw them some sweets . . .

Boom!

Good God! That was too close!

Helmet – grabbed. Machine gun – ready. *Crash!* The truck swerved and rammed the vehicle in front. Many voices shouted at once.

'What's happened?' he hissed to Erich.

'Sabotage? Mines buried in the road . . . Italian partisans, throwing explosives under the wheels? God knows. Treacherous swine can't even wait for the Allies to land before they start stabbing us in the back. How's that for gratitude? One minute we're their best defence against the enemy, now we *are* the enemy. See anything behind us?'

Peter dropped to his belly, pushed the tailboard of the truck down and looked along the sights of his gun. What could he see? Clouds of dust. A road clogged with vehicles, and strange lumps crouching in the ditch at the roadside. What were they? People? Women, mostly, some kids. Skinny wretches, all of them. No reason to lower his weapon or relax his aim. Any one of them could be a guerrilla fighter, ready to rise out of the ditch to attack . . . So be it. He looked along the gun sights. The *Fallschirmjäger* ninth commandment was clear on how to respond: *Against an open foe, fight with chivalry, but to a guerrilla extend no quarter*.

Erich shifted position and peered ahead.

'Was it a mine?' Peter murmured, finger poised on the trigger.

'I don't think so . . . Hell!' Erich began to laugh. 'The tyre on the truck in front has blown, that's all!'

'All clear!' cried Corporal Mahler. 'Stretch your legs while they change tyres, but keep alert.'

Just as Peter prepared to rise he saw a soldier in the next truck along get up and begin to climb over his mates, saying, 'Shift it, boys, I'm dying for a leak.' Then the air cracked and the soldier's head jerked back. A spray of red mixed with the haze of brown dust. The soldier slumped over the side of the truck.

Peter's world contracted to the sense of pressure on his trigger finger and a line of sweat running out from under his helmet. *It wasn't me!* he thought. *I never even fired!* Several minutes passed. A lizard darted across the road. Blood dripped. Word spread: another false alarm. The lad had accidentally shot himself while scrambling about.

'Schoolboy error,' said Erich, but his voice wasn't entirely steady. He crouched at Peter's side. 'Stupid idiot forgot to put the safety on. Don't worry, it's no one we know. Come on – time to fill a pipe while they sort the tyre puncture.'

Peter couldn't help staring at the corpse. He was very conscious of his own heart beating and blood running through his body. One second. That's all it took to change from alive to dead. Where had the life gone? Into the gritty air? He looked for a shimmer, a wisp, some sort of spirit perhaps. The only wisp he saw was the trace of steam at the summit of Vesuvius. A man died and the world seemed the same as ever, just another sunny September afternoon.

Dying for a leak. Who'd want those as their last words?

Gun slung over one shoulder – safety on – he jumped down from the truck and took a few steps, just to see if he had changed somehow after seeing his first death. A new noise made him look skywards where a solitary fighter plane flew high above the blue sea – too far away to waste bullets on.

'RAF Spitfire,' said Heini. He was always like that, seeing things, knowing things, shooting on target.

The Spitfire was soon challenged by a German Focke-wulfe 190. The planes flew in a graceful duet, circling, climbing, diving, until a distant shot ended the dogfight. There was a flare of light and a billowing cloud of black smoke tumbled from the Spitfire's engine. Slowly its nose dipped down. It began to dive, spinning a corkscrew of smoke. The crash, when it came, was too far away to witness. Water doused the burning pilot.

Peter blinked. Another mental postcard picture of war. At least this was something he could write home about. Erich said it was a lucky omen of things to come, hey they were going to win the war, after all. Heini said he didn't believe in luck but skill. Was he right? What about Lanky, kissing his silver St Christopher medal? Or Jupp, flashing a picture of a nude cabaret girl, saying it was Lady Luck in person. Did a diary count as a good luck charm, even if it had been stolen?

'I saw Corporal Mahler with a lucky rabbit foot,' he said.

'Not so lucky for the rabbit!' Erich mocked. He tore open a ration pack. 'I wonder if that lad who just blew his head to bolognese sauce had one. Tell you what, we need a mascot.'

Just as he said this a very dirty dog scrambled out of the ditch at the side of the road and cannoned into Erich's legs, barking for food.

Peter's first instinct was to shoot, then he relaxed and laughed. 'Give it a bit of breakfast. Yours, not mine.'

Erich tossed it half a biscuit. The dog's ribs moved under its wiry grey fur, it was so skinny. A few more bribes had it licking Erich's boots and rolling around to have a scabby tummy tickled.

'He's grinning,' Erich laughed.

Peter frowned. 'He looks familiar . . .'

Surely it couldn't be the same scruffy mutt he'd chased from the marina in Naples? Surely that couldn't actually be Vittoria Venafro down there in the ditch – that dust-streaked, bramble-scratched, sunburnt creature? After all this time he hadn't expected to see her again.

She lifted her head and looked right at him. Her gaze was so angry he almost took a step backwards. She flung

91

down the basket she'd been holding and began yelling at the dog, *'Zecca! Zecca! Veni, pronto!'*

Zecca had to be the dog's name – whatever *Zecca* meant in Italian.

'Asking for trouble,' said Heini, stubbing out his cigarette. He swung his gun off his shoulder.

Erich nearly choked on his pipe. 'Is that the girl who fleeced us?'

'Let me go first.' Slowly Peter approached the ditch. *'Meine buch!'* he called angrily.

'Meine hunde!' Vittoria shouted back.

'*Your* dog? You're not fit to own an animal if you starve it like that.'

'He eats better than we do!'

'What are you doing in the ditch? Put your hands up where I can see them! Step away from that basket.'

She did move, but only to shield a huddle of children who were hiding in her shadow as if her slender body was any kind of protection from soldiers with machine guns.

'Take a look if you like!' she taunted. 'It's weeds, mostly, for soup.'

He stared at the wilting greens. Had he understood her German right? They'd walked all this way to pick *dandelions*? It had to be at least eight miles back to

Naples. Looking along the ditch, Peter saw all the women and children were busy gleaning whatever plants they could find.

Vittoria scowled. 'Yes, pathetic, isn't it? What did you think we would eat when you put barbed wire round all the fields and leave the harvest to rot?'

He had no answer for that.

'*Mi libro!*' he shouted again, in his newly learned Italian.

In reply she copied the British Prime Minister. She gave him Winston Churchill's famous two-fingered *Victory* salute. Backwards.

The convoy rumbled to life again. Erich spat his reply into the dust. 'Stuck-up peasant. Leave her, Turnip. Come on – we've got medals to win.' He tossed a few crumpled notes of Italian money into the ditch then bundled the dog into the truck, declaring, 'Spoils of war! I'm going to call him Winston.'

The soldiers grinned. Now they had a mascot – their own good luck charm. They felt immortal.

Tyre tracks obliterated the patch of red blood on the road.

Peter watched Vittoria grow smaller and smaller as the trucks moved on.

The Rules of War

I just love getting letters.

I know texts and emails are great. I know lots of baby trees are brutally hacked up to make paper and that's bad. I *know* there's no one (hardly) who writes to me. Doesn't mean I don't feel skippity-skip when I see something oblong on the doormat (unless it's just a new telephone directory or a pizza menu or an ad for a bloke who cleans windows or a note saying someone called to read the meter).

We got a letter from Rich!

Mum was working when it arrived so I took it next door, since Craig had already beetled off there before the letter came, mumbling something about taking Winnie for a walk.

I found him with the Shepherds in their kitchen. Dr

Shepherd was dusting, well, moving a yellow cloth over all the junk. Those eight shiny bullets on the spice rack, she picked them up one by one and put them back in a row. It would have been asking for trouble – and a long monologue – if I'd asked her what they were doing there, so I kept my mouth shut. She pretended to dust Mr Shepherd, who was polishing his boots.

'A letter from your brother?' he asked. Mr S didn't talk much – probably couldn't get a word in edgewise when Dr S was on a roll. He had a nice warm voice and a slight accent.

Craig squawked, 'Read it, read it!'

'It might be private,' I said.

'Rubbish,' said Craig. 'We always share Rich's letters. Isn't it to everyone?'

I ripped the envelope open. Yup. It started *Dear All* . . .

I told the Shepherds they might think it was boring since they didn't know our brother.

Mr Shepherd looked at his wife and smiled. Loon.

I read:

Dear All,
Thanks for the parcel – v glad to get it all, esp the bog roll + books. Not much time to read right now tho. Lots going on. Beats being bored. Boom box is bust but we get radio. It's a

good bunch of lads so there's always loads of laughs.

Right near the place where we doss there's a camel spider hangs out. Nasty big b-ggers they are, poisonous too, except they can't kill humans. Stumpy's dead scared of spiders so he took a jerry can of petrol and emptied half into this spider's hole – they dig in the ground. He set fire to the petrol and we got this horrible burning smell . . . black smoke's coming from the hole and Stumpy's cheering, then the smoke cleared and out came this <u>really</u> hacked-off spider . . . You should've seen Stumpy's face, he nearly cakked himself on the spot.

Hope you're all ok. You seen anyone driving my car round town? Still gutted I had to sell that old rust bucket. Heard from Mum you're doing cross-country, Craig. Are u in training for the paras? Gonna sign up n join me here??!! Denise – bet you're jealous I'm getting a tan.

So everything's groovy here. I got a full water bottle n dry feet – living the dream! Sorry about the spelling n that. Write soon if u like.

Luv, Rich.

No kiss.

'Stumpy's his mate,' Craig explained. 'Like Peter and Erich.'

I asked, 'Who's Erich when he's at home?'

'Erich Bergen, in Peter's platoon. They trained and fought together. Mates are important. Like me and Tariq.'

'Tariq's a squirt.'

'He's joined cross-country too so now I'm not the slowest.'

Mr Shepherd set his boots straight.

'The bonds between men who fight are very strong,' he said quietly. 'Your life might depend on the man next to you.'

Craig nodded. 'The *Fallschirmjäger* second commandment is . . .' (fish fish fish for the grotty piece of paper he'd gone and written them all out on . . .) '*Cultivate true comradeship, for by the aid of your comrades you will conquer or die.*'

Or die.

NOT something Rich was allowed to do. Since Sam Green's outburst in the changing rooms, saying Rich was a baby-butcher-war-criminal, I wasn't all that happy with the idea of him conquering either. People got killed in Afghanistan. Was Richard doing any shooting? Maybe he was just on guard duty, or patrols, things like that. I read the letter again. *Lots going on.* What sort of *lots*? Before he left he boasted he could strip a rifle in twenty-five seconds and reassemble it in the dark, so that's not going to take up too much of his time, is it?

'Rich never actually says anything about where he is or what he's doing,' I complained.

Mr Shepherd said this was because soldiers live in a different world. Not a nice one. Not one they want to share with their families.

Dr Shepherd snorted. 'You talk as if war is two armies of soldiers in a field, smart uniforms, tall hats, swords and horses, only fighting each other. Stupidity! War is *not* a different world! It happens in the world normal people live in. It happens to civilians. To families.'

Craig butted in. 'Rich says they do their best to avoid casualties in Afghanistan. They're there to protect people. To stop terrorists. That saves lives.'

'Yes yes, that's what politicians say but Afghanistan is full of ordinary people too. Children! How can they be kept safe in the middle of a war?'

'There are rules of war,' said Craig.

She flapped her duster at him. 'Rules? The only rule in war is survive if you can. Do you think bombs or bullets obey rules?'

Mr Shepherd touched his wife's arm and she stopped flailing around. He could see that Craig was getting upset, even if she was too het up to notice. I was getting pretty antsy about it all myself. Why can't things just be Right or Wrong? Why didn't the Bad Guys have big sticky labels on their heads saying, I'm Evil So It's OK To Blow My Brains Out?

'It's just all a big mess!' I said suddenly, without meaning to.

Mr Shepherd nodded.

Craig wasn't done though. He was thinking hard – you could practically see steam coming out of his ears.

'About war,' he started. 'It's, like, really destructive and people die and you can't decide who and stuff.'

'What a master of eloquence,' I muttered.

'No listen, Dr Shepherd's right. War's all wrong. Except, sometimes you have to do it, don't you? I mean, it'd be cool if you had these smart bombs that only splatted the enemy, not, you know, innocent people. Except there aren't any, not till scientists invent them in the future, which would be *really* cool, except they haven't yet, so we have to go and invade places and people die, you can't help that.' He stopped to take breath.

'Or you could just let people sort out their own problems instead of barging in and blowing things up,' I said.

'Yeah, like that would've been a great idea in World War Two. Let's just leave Hitler to wipe out everyone he wanted to in Europe because it's not our problem.'

Mr Shepherd nodded. 'The great Roman lawyer

Cicero said, *The only excuse for war is that we may live in peace unharmed.*'

'Totally. I mean, the Allies seriously *had* to invade – even a complete *dimbo* knows that – so they could kill the Nazis, even though tens of thousands of people eventually died trying to destroy Hitler's empire.'

'Tens of thousands still died defending it,' growled Dr Shepherd.

'That is what soldiers do, Vicky,' Mr Shepherd said quietly. They follow orders. They fight for what they believe in – or what they're told to believe in. Even the German ones.'

'Like Peter Schäfer,' said Craig.

Mr Shepherd sort of smiled. 'Yes, as you say, like Peter Schäfer. Please – don't worry about your brother. I am sure Richard Cooper is a good man. He'll be doing his job as best he can.'

Dr Shepherd slumped on to a creaky kitchen stool. I swear she wanted to carry on arguing. I bet she was dying to come up with something like, *Richard Cooper's job is killing people.* Because that's exactly what I was starting to think, in a nasty, secret part of my mind. My mental knickers were getting in a serious twist! Time for a complete change of subject before World War Three started in the kitchen of number sixty-four Willow Garth.

I looked around. Cupboards, dishes, curtains, spice rack, eight shiny bullets in a row . . .

'You were telling us before about that girl in Naples – Vittoria. About how she stole some treasure.'

Dr Shepherd stopped grumbling and sat upright. 'Stole? No, she *found* that treasure on the beach at Herculaneum. You received my message about it?'

Message?

'I posted it to you,' she added with a sniff.

'Oh, we got the envelope with the coin.'

'Yes, exactly. My message.'

I felt myself going pink. It was just about the utter pits of embarrassment. I could see Mr Shepherd was uncomfortable too. My diversion tactic was going horribly wrong. I had *no idea* what she was talking about.

'I'm sorry, I don't understand. What's the coin for?'

'Four? No, there were five all together. Five gold coins. Some with the head of Nero, some with Vespasian, who was emperor just before Vesuvius erupted.'

Craig said, 'We figured it was a Roman coin. A replica, obviously.'

'Replica? You mean, a fake? No, no, stupidity! It is a real golden *aureus*, the most expensive Roman coin. Gold is always precious, and dangerous too. It changes the brain, you see, makes people a little lunatic I think. It was

101

a big risk for Vittoria to show that gold on the Via Forcella, to exchange it for things she needed. Via Forcella was the heart of the black market in Naples. Here you could buy anything, *anything*, no questions. Even when people starved and babies cried because there was no milk, Via Forcella was a street of abundance. Why are you squinting at me, Craig? You don't know what is a black market?'

'Yeah I do. It's illegal trading. Dodgy dealings. Under the counter.'

She tried the new word out. 'Dodgy? Yes. A dodgy market, with dodgy men and sometimes dodgy death as a punishment. Of course, it was better when the Allies landed and the Germans left Naples.'

'Where'd they go?'

'The Germans? Italy decided to changed sides, because it looked as if the Allies might win. Too late for that! As if the Germans would just, how do you say, click their heels and go home? Of course not!'

Craig nodded, as if he was some brainbox military expert. 'They'd have to stay and occupy Italy because they couldn't let the Allies march up Italy closer to Germany.'

'Correct. That is why the German paratroopers were there, fighting to defend every field, every valley, every mountain . . .'

'. . . to the death,' finished Mr Shepherd gravely.

Dr Shepherd frowned at him.

'What happened?' Craig asked.

She sighed. 'What happened? The Allied invasion of southern Italy was a success. Naples was liberated. Many hundreds had to die, but *c'est la guerre*, as they say – that's war. In the first days of October the Allies drove into town smiling and waving, as if everything would be fine.'

'Wasn't it?'

Bless him. Craig wanted some storybook Hollywood version, where the flags come out and everyone sings one of those wartime songs, like 'Roll Out the Barrel', or 'We'll Meet Again', la la la Happy Ending.

Actually, that's *exactly* the sort of thing I wanted to happen, too. I didn't like the way Dr Shepherd's face was crinkling up, all sad. I wanted to put my hands over my ears . . . and at the same time I wanted to hear everything that happened.

She said, 'Fine? How could it be fine? This was only autumn 1943, remember. Only just were the Allies starting to win significant battles. Nearly two years more of war they had to endure. The Germans, they were not giving up without a fight. It was terrible, what the Nazis did before they left Naples. The historical library – all burned. The water supply – spoiled. Food taken.

Artworks and treasures taken. No rules, no rules at all.'

'My dear, some things were taken to keep safe,' said Mr Shepherd. 'Objects from Naples Museum.'

'Oh yes. You want me to say about the treasures at Monte Cassino monastery? Here is where many artefacts were stored, Roman treasures from Herculaneum and Pompeii and many others, moved miles away from the invasion. Not far enough! All had to be moved again as the Allies made battle through Italy, pushing the Germans north. *We are taking things to Rome*, the German officer said – Lieutenant-Colonel Julius Schlegel. Also he took treasures from the monastery. A very rich place, you understand, this old monastery of Monte Cassino, with many statues and paintings. Tintoretto, Raphael, Titian, Brueghel, the best names in art, all packed into trucks by German soldiers. They filmed the removal with movie cameras, you know.'

I asked, 'Why?'

That earned me a classic *Do You Even Have a Brain*? look from the old lady.

'For propaganda,' she said. 'To show the German people appreciate *Kultur*. This film I have seen.'

'And Monte Cassino library . . .' Mr Shepherd prompted. 'That was saved too.'

'Yes! I will tell them about the library. One hundred

thousand books taken from the monastery to Rome. The Germans burn one library and save another. Is there a rule for that, tell me?'

Mr Shepherd seemed keen to put a different spin on it. He said, 'The monastery was in danger of being bombed by the Allies.'

'Only because the Germans were defending it . . .'

'It was an important strategic position! What else would the army do? At least the treasures were moved, for safety, as Schlegel said.' Mr Shepherd's voice softened. 'You two children are too young to understand about the library . . .'

(I HATE it when people say that. Usually because they're about to spout something I don't actually understand in the slightest.)

'It was such a special place. Some of the books there were many centuries old. More than that, the monastery had ten thousand parchment rolls of works by great Roman writers – Cicero, Horace, Ovid, Virgil, Seneca . . .'

'You said Peter Schäfer knew those writers,' said Craig, as if a light had just gone on in his head.

Mr Shepherd waved his hand. '*Ach*, never mind about Peter.'

Dr Shepherd pinched her husband's arm. 'You are late for your rehearsal, yes? I will help me with your coat.

Your case is by the door, see, and your shoes are polished. All ready for you to go.'

'I don't need to leave yet,' he objected.

'Then *sss*! Let me tell this story. Where was I?'

'The monastery place,' prompted Craig.

'Monte Cassino. Yes, Peter and Erich were there too. Terrible luck for them but, I admit it, fortunate all those books and treasures were removed, when you remember what happened in 1944 . . .'

(Remember? I was pretty certain I'd never known!)

'*What* happened?' Craig asked.

I interrupted before Dr Shepherd could go rambling off again. I wanted to know about the treasure.

'What about the gold coins? What about Vittoria and the Allies and the black market?'

'Yes, dear,' said Mr Shepherd. 'Tell them about Vittoria, why don't you?'

Dr Shepherd glared. 'I will if you don't interrupt! Can you reach to fasten your shoelaces?'

'I can reach,' he said with a ghost of a smile as he bent to tie them.

Dr Shepherd absent-mindedly wiped her nose on the yellow duster. 'Well, in October the Allies came into Naples and the *scugnizzi* were so happy!'

'Because they'd been liberated?'

'Because the Allies were easy for stealing! Their food, their uniforms, the tyres off their trucks. It was all for sale on the dodgy market, *facilissimo*. And the Allies didn't shoot so many people as the Germans. They wanted to help civilians, where possible.'

Then a shadow fell across her face.

'The Germans were gone from the town but they left, how do you say, *souvenirs* . . . The water, the stealing, you know about this. But they left bombs too. Bombs ticking on timers.'

I couldn't believe this sort of stuff. 'You're not winding us up? The Germans really booby-trapped the town even when they'd had to retreat?'

Dr Shepherd didn't reply. Her lips were a thin, tight line.

Mr Shepherd took her hand.

'Yes they did,' he said. 'It was a terrible thing. The Germans were gone but they did not want to be forgotten. The truth is, sometimes the only rules of war are the ones that are broken in order to try and win. Cicero said it best: *In time of war the laws are silent.*'

The Post Office Bomb

October 1943

Vittoria had one thought as she walked to the post office on that crisp October morning, one thought only: *Let there be a letter*!

Liberation was old news. One set of soldiers had replaced another. Now, instead of American bombers pounding the city, German planes came most evenings. True, the Allies were friendly on the whole, and they were fighting fascism, but the important thing was to know if mail was getting through from Rome, where the Germans were still in control. The Contessa said it was silly to keep waiting for letters when none ever came.

Vittoria wouldn't listen to her. Where there's life there's hope.

Let there be a letter . . . Just one letter from her mama and papa, telling her all was well, that they'd be home soon, that they'd come and take care of her.

She stayed in the shady side of the street, arm plastered across her satchel to keep it safe. It was comforting to know that no matter how bad things got – and they were bad – she still had five gold coins to sell. *If* she could work up the courage to show them to anyone. *If* she dared believe they were real. Each time she opened the leather purse she expected to see they'd vanished as abruptly as the strange soldier she'd imagined on that beach at Herculaneum.

The post office was jammed with people all demanding the impossible – order out of chaos. She elbowed her way to the counter. If nothing else, the Contessa had taught her how to get where she wanted with her nose in the air. The clerk was an oldish man with a head rising turtle-like from his stiff, greasy collar.

'Yes, miss?'

'Is there any mail from Rome?'

'No. Nothing.'

'Could you go and check?'

'No.'

'Why not?'

'Because I already know I won't find any.'

A bird-thin lady in combat trousers and a fur coat tapped Vittoria on the shoulder. 'There's nothing for you here, let me through.'

'But I'm expecting letters from my parents!'

The clerk muttered, 'Don't hold your breath.'

'I would if mine stank like yours!'

The fur-coat lady started grumbling, and that set others off. Vittoria didn't care about that, but she wouldn't let them see any tears in her eyes. She marched straight outside with her head high, just like a queen ought.

Barely half a minute later the bomb exploded.

Time stopped.

Sound was sucked away.

Vittoria whirled through the street, with stones flying round her like a scene in a giant snow globe. There was sky, there was ground, neither where it ought to be. Then she couldn't see, couldn't hear, could only feel warmth pouring from her head and down her face. Tasted blood. Choked on dust. Opened her eyes to a grey world peopled with statues stuck in the last stiff pose of **death, like the plaster-casts of volcano victims in**

Pompeii. The world was grey, all grey, no colour anywhere. Screams began, high and loud, bizarrely far away and close at the same time.

She covered her ears.

Dear God in heaven with all the angels playing harps with halos and feathered wings! There'd been no planes! No warning! Where had this bomb come from? Would there be more? Why was there a burning hole where the post office had been?

She had to leave but couldn't move.

Someone touched her arm. She flinched.

'You are hurt?' asked a voice.

Of course not. Perhaps. 'Yes, my head. It's sticky.'

'Here.'

Her fingers grasped something soft. Automatically she reached up and pressed it to a cut on her head. Would her blood run out grey too?

Click. *Flash!*

'Permit me . . . I can take a photograph? My name is Margaret Bentley-Wyke. Photojournalist. Forgive me. I speak . . . I don't speak . . . Italian not very good. I am England. I mean, English.'

Who was this woman? Her name was too hard to understand. Margaret Something-Something. The words sounded like mangled metal. She was very smartly dressed with boxy shoulders on her wool suit, sensible ankle boots and hair neatly rolled, just like Mama's.

Where is my mama? Why doesn't she pick me up and kiss it better?

The woman produced a notebook and pencil.

'What is your name? Are you alone? I write in newspaper . . . *for* a newspaper. I write about children. In war. You understand – the war?'

Understand war? Vittoria watched the street scene as calmly as if she were seeing a film at the cinema.

Panic-stricken mothers, soldiers, sailors, nurses, everyone turned grey in seconds as they ran to the street. It was like a new uniform anyone could wear. They began to scrabble in the rubble.

It's no use looking, Vittoria thought. *There aren't any letters*.

'Here's one alive!' came the call. A grey shape with arms and legs was pulled into daylight, gulping like a fish without water. She saw lumps of things that must have been people once, just a few moments before. She blinked. What were those wisps of grey hanging over each dead body? They had faces distorted with pain and hands reaching, imploring . . .

No. Her sight cleared, the vision passed. There were no ghosts. The bodies were just bodies. Ash began to settle.

A new fear made her frantic. Where was her satchel? The gold?

Relief. Still strapped across her body. Still safe.

The journalist was still talking, something about war being terrible . . . bad for women . . . bad for children . . . the innocents. Information: she was staying at a field hospital in Naples, the sixty-seventh . . . she could help . . . she had chocolate. Questions: where is your father . . . is he a soldier . . . what were the Germans like . . . are you hungry . . .?

Too many questions!

Click. *Flash!* More photographs.

'Here, I help you . . .' Margaret raised Vittoria to her feet.

Gently, gently, Vittoria acquired the woman's slender gold wristwatch, a crocodile leather wallet and a few rolls of spare camera film. That was pure instinct.

Now she had one thought and one thought only: *There weren't any letters from Rome.*

She shook the journalist off. Somehow her legs walked her home. Nonna was nowhere to be seen. The Contessa waited on the first-floor landing.

'Vittoria! Look at you! Did you come through the streets like that? Is there blood in your hair? Are you hurt? What will people think? Put your hand over your mouth when you cough. Wash at once and come to the salon. That serving girl from the bakery was here – Nina Dragone. She said letters have been smuggled out of Rome. *Finally* there is news of your parents.'

Remembrance Sunday

We were supposed to go on a day trip to the seaside, which is madness in November, I know, but it's not often Mum gets a Sunday off, so we dug out our raincoats and hunted for the car keys, then Mum suddenly stopped dead and closed her eyes, saying she'd completely forgotten it was Sunday. *The* Sunday. Remembrance Day.

I was seriously unimpressed. 'You can't make us stand through another Remembrance Service! It goes on for ever and there's always one old veteran who collapses and they have to get the ambulance. Can't I go shopping and meet you after? I hate it when they fire the cannon.'

'You just hate having to stay quiet for the minute's silence,' Craig said.

'Quiet, both of you,' said Mum. 'Denise, stop being so difficult. You know perfectly well why we're going.'

Fine. We went. Got there in time to see the last of the veterans marching to a halt by the stone memorial. Not many people about. You'd have to be insane to leave the sofa on such a cold day in November. We were all scrunched deep in our coats.

'It's freeeeezing,' I moaned.

Craig went all airy. 'Not as cold as Italy in winter. The German paratroopers were in the mountains, getting attacked by the Allies. It was so cold they actually had to pee on their machine guns to stop them freezing.'

'That's gross.'

'Yeah, but not really, cos the *Fallschirmjäger* seventh commandment says you can only triumph if your weapons are good. They made shelters out of rocks because it was too cold to dig the ground. Mr Shepherd says it wasn't how you think of war at all . . .'

'You're right, I don't think of war at all.'

'Seriously, it wasn't all hero stuff and explosions. Actually, the soldiers got frostbite, which is where your fingers and toes go black and sometimes they snap off . . .'

'For God's sake, Craig!'

'*Plus* they got fleas and lice and something called scabies. Erich's dog Winston – their mascot – he had big nits. Ticks. They had to burn them off with lit cigarettes.'

'Nice.' Not. 'You're obsessed with those German paras. You don't know when to stop.'

'I do! But listen, mice ate their rations and rats ate everything else. There wasn't any firewood in the mountains and it snowed every day, real blizzards, so Winston kept them warm at night. When they were being fired on they couldn't leave the shelters, even for the loo. Did you know they had to crap on their spades and chuck it out?'

'No I didn't and funnily enough I haven't been losing sleep about that detail of history. Who's been telling you all this stuff, no, wait, I get it. Dr Shepherd.'

'Mr Shepherd actually. Did you know . . . ?'

'No! Shut up. I don't care.'

'Be like that then!'

He stomped off in a huff and went to stand near the kids from the cadet forces. The proper Royal Air Force were there too, and the Navy and the Army, all in uniforms. It was funny, but the old duffers from the war looked smarter than the nowadays lot. All these veterans had a ton of medals, even the women.

Craig didn't once look back at me and Mum. What was wrong with him? What was wrong with *me*? I was blank on the outside, but all seething and churned up inside, like hot lava in a volcano, waiting to erupt.

I scrunched deeper in my coat.

Remembrance Sunday. What on earth was I supposed to remember? The big wars all happened before I was born. There was Dad, of course. Not that I can remember ANYTHING about him. I was really little when he left for the Gulf. Would there be a memorial to him one day – Staff Sergeant Steve Cooper?

It was crazy, but I sort of found myself looking for Dad's face, as if he'd be standing with the other soldiers. Even crazier, I thought I saw him, a glimpse of him, looking like he does in the photo next to Mum's bed – smiling and alive. Then it wasn't just Dad who somehow appeared in the mizzly rain. I'm not kidding. As I stood there, fingering the gold coin in my coat pocket, I actually thought I saw a whole crowd of grey people, some standing to attention between the ranks of uniforms, some huddled behind the crowd of normal people. Grey people, grey faces, grey eyes staring . . .

Dad's face slid down with the rain. His mouth drooped and opened. No sounds came out but I heard words all the same: *Can you help?*

Blink.

No Dad.

I shivered. Closed and opened my eyes. Rubbed a couple of stupid tears away.

The band marched off, trailing everyone behind. I suddenly noticed Dr Shepherd and her hubby, both setting a wreath on the memorial steps. She was wearing a hat covered in rainbows and her scarf was a glitzy cascade of fluff with sequins. Nothing grey about her.

She waved to me and came over, leaving Mr S – who looked a bit grim, I thought – to chat with some veterans.

'Are you all packed?' she asked cheerfully.

I was still a bit spaced from my crazy hallucination. *Packed?* Did she mean for our seaside trip? How could she even know about that? Her next words made even less sense: 'You will go to Monte Cassino and Herculaneum. Perhaps the mountain will burn again. They often say, *See Naples and die.*'

Naples? Die?? Was she absolutely out of her tree?

'Are you . . . Shall I . . . I'll just see where my mum is,' I stammered, thinking I ought to go drag Mr Shepherd over and ask if he kept a straitjacket for this sort of loony moment.

'Now listen,' Dr Shepherd said calmly. 'I am taking my husband to hospital for a few days. Winnie will be in the kennels, she hates it, but what can we do? When we come back we can start making plans, when you'll go, where you'll stay, things like that. You have to go before it is too late. *Do you understand?* Time is running out! You're

119

young, you have plenty. Me, my husband, we are, how do you say, *borrowing* it. Always when you are borrowing things you must return them.'

I want to say she sounded bonkers. (Well, she did!) She also had this utterly, totally *true* feeling about her, I can't explain it. Otherwise why would I even have been standing there listening?

Then the old lady sort of snapped out of her funny mood because my mum rolled up to introduce herself.

'Hi, I'm Emma Cooper from next door. Nice to meet you in person. I keep meaning to pop round and say thanks for fixing the back door, but there's always something, you know how it is. Anyway, I'm glad so many people have turned out today.'

'Fewer every year,' said Dr Shepherd. 'The singing is very bad and I don't like all the prayers, but it suits some people.'

Mum went all stiff. 'I see. Well, *we* think Remembrance Sunday is a very important tradition, don't we?'

Craig was back. He blurted out, 'Dad's a war hero. Can I take Winnie for a walk this afternoon, now we're not going to the seaside?'

'Hardly a hero,' I said. 'He got run over by a drunk driver on the Basra highway when I was only three. It wasn't even during any fighting, it was after the first Gulf War was *over*.'

How dare you? said Mum's expression.

Dr Shepherd's eyes narrowed. 'There is more to a hero than shooting and bombing.'

So then I felt really bad . . . but angry-bad. I couldn't stop mean words spewing out.

'He didn't exactly sacrifice his life for his country like the vicar was saying in the speeches just now.'

Mum was almost crying, it was awful. 'Of course it was a sacrifice! He didn't want to leave. I was pregnant with Craig and you were only little and Richard missed his dad, and Steve was sent halfway round the world to a war everyone wanted to forget about. He went and did his duty. He was a hero.'

'Mum! He was a *chef*, for God's sake!'

'That's enough from you!'

'Fine. I didn't want to come here anyway.'

I was, I don't know, angry. Really churned-up angry. Mad that I was supposed to feel all holy and *meaningful* on Remembrance Day. Mad I didn't have a dad to remember properly. Mad that I actually did feel really pigging SAD for some reason.

Dr Shepherd didn't help. She said, 'You should remember your father. At least the soldiers, they are remembered. They have the brass bands and the names

121

written on these, these ... stone monuments. What about the Iraqis who are dead in the Gulf wars? All the civilians ... they are suffering in every war ... Who remembers them?'

She fumbled in her coat pocket and pulled a picture out. I kind of recognised it from the pile of junk she'd shown us that first time we went round and saw the *Fallschirmjäger* insignia. It was the torn-off cover of an old magazine, showing a black-and-white picture of a girl in the middle of some bomb blast, with a hanky soaking up blood from this big gash in her head. The headline at the bottom of the picture was, *Naples Post Office Bomb – the True Face of War*.

'Look – that is what war is,' she said in a shaky voice.

'War's awful,' said Mum, just as shaky, 'but we're not ashamed to remember the men and women who go and fight for their country, who sacrifice their lives in whatever way.'

Dr Shepherd folded her picture up again. 'I sometimes think the dead are the lucky ones. Their suffering, it is over. Those who live, they are forgotten but they have the memories of everything they've seen.'

She seized her husband's hand. He'd just come over. He didn't say anything. He really did look pretty ill. I hoped he wasn't going to be the token pensioner who keeled over and conked out.

Mum said, 'If you must know, my oldest son Richard's a paratrooper in the army and I'm proud of what he does. In fact, I came here today to pray he keeps safe. I'm sorry you're so against the ceremony.'

Now Dr Shepherd's anger cleared and she blinked. 'Me? Not at all. We come every year. After, we always visit that lovely café on the bridge, for tea and cake. You will join us now, yes? Our present to you?'

Apparently not.

Mum dragged me and Craig away saying, 'I don't know if I like that woman. You're not to go talking to her again, except to be polite.'

'Can't I walk Winnie this afternoon?'

'No, Craig, you can't, well, unless you promised you would, I suppose.'

Craig winked at me and whispered, 'I'll see if I can find out more about that gold money when I go round.'

Find out *more*? I didn't want to know more. I didn't want to know *anything* right then. I just wanted to get away from everyone and yell. Why were things so . . . stupid? So complicated? The more I knew, the less I understood. A paratrooper's insignia, a gold coin, Naples, Monte Cassino . . . what the bloody hell did they all have in common? And what did they have to do with me?

123

Epidemic

October 1943

Vittoria sat crumpled on the salon carpet, lit by a square of speckled sunlight.

Arrested?

How could this be the news she'd been waiting for? There had to be some mistake. The Contessa was speaking, it seemed. Her red lips were moving. Her tongue was pink. Vittoria couldn't hear a word, not with all the echoes of bombs blasting in her head.

She stared at the letter instead. The letter that had finally arrived. Black words on white paper.

Arrested. Mama in prison. Papa last seen on train crammed with Jews, destination Auschwitz.

Auschwitz?

What sort of place was Auschwitz? Trains went there full and came back empty.

She waited, waited, waited. Waited for Mama to come and tell her not to worry, everything would be all right.

A glass of something heady and sweet-smelling waved under her nose.

'Drink this, you've had a shock,' the Contessa said.

'I'm half-Jewish,' Vittoria whispered. 'Will they arrest me too?'

'Arrest my niece? Impossible! The Germans are gone from Naples now. I have new connections amongst the Allied officers. They will take care of us. But, if we are to be sensible – and we must be sensible – we have to consider that it might not be safe here, not for Jews. Perhaps you should go, I am not sure where. Your father's family in Venafro, perhaps? No, they may have been arrested too. It's too exasperating! Why did my sister have to marry a Jew of all people! Listen, pack your clothes – you have a suitcase, don't you? – and come back in a while, when things are calmer.'

Arrested. Auschwitz.

The Contessa began to flit about the salon touching things, picking them up, setting them down. A brandy decanter. An embroidered cushion. Pages of music from the piano.

125

'I haven't any money to give you, you know that. Take this brooch. It was your mother's. I never liked it much, and see, it has left two holes on my dress and I can hardly afford to buy a new one. Oh, for the love of heaven, stop crying. Remember who you are! Whatever your father's heritage, you still have Sanfelice blood running in your veins.'

Running down my cheek from the cut on my head . . .

'It wouldn't be for long. Only until all this . . . disturbance . . . is over. You are sixteen now. Old enough to take care of yourself.'

'Fifteen. I'm almost fifteen.'

'At fifteen I was nearly engaged to be married – God rest my husband's soul. Careful! Don't mark the chairs – you're covered in dust.'

I don't know where to go.

Vittoria got to her feet. The salon seemed . . . *wrong* somehow. The furniture kept moving. The walls were sliding sideways. It wasn't safe. She had to get out. Leave. Now.

'Vittoria! Come back here now! Where are you going?' The Contessa's voice began to unravel. Casa Sanfelice began to fall into rubble and ruin. The earth shook.

No. The ground was steady and Vittoria was the one

shaking. She was out in the courtyard at the back of the house, holding on to the rough plaster wall for support. If her legs hadn't been so weak she would have been walking, no, running to the station, catching a train, heading to Rome, going to Auschwitz, finding her mama, finding her papa, leaving the strays, the bombs, the whole wretched town behind . . .

She wasn't crying, more like gulping every breath down as if the air was running out. Her mama wasn't coming! Her papa wasn't coming! There was no one to help.

'Who's there?'

The sun was too bright. Her eyes were dazzled. Even squinting she couldn't see clearly. Was that a man sitting by the broken water pump? The soldier Justinius! Had he come for his gold?

He rose and walked towards her. He cast no shadow. As before, on Herculaneum beach, she struggled to understand his words at first. Then they fell into her mind and echoed there.

You are not alone. Can you help?

Help? How could he even ask it, when she was so helpless herself?

Someone pulled at her dress. A cloud covered the sun and Justinius was gone. She looked down.

'Diavolo! We're not working today, I told you.'

Diavolo was there with his little sister, Doll. Hovering behind were Anna-Maria and her cousin Tonio. With them were three more children, all bones and rags.

What?! she raged silently. *What do you want from me now? Haven't I done enough? I know you're hungry! I know you're sleeping on the streets! What can I do?*

Everything had changed . . . nothing had changed. There would be more bombs, more air raids, more bad news. Winter would bite. They'd need firewood. Blankets. Food. Water for drinking and washing . . . Dear God in heaven with all the angels playing harps in halos with feathery wings and white gowns . . . there was still *so much* to do!

Diavolo tugged at her dress again.

'Vittoria, my head hurts.'

'That's your brain growing.'

She pressed her palm to his forehead. It was very hot. Was he ill? Please God, no. There was no mama to run to for medicine, kisses and kind words. Nonna would know what to do. Nonna would help.

Nonna was in her dim, windowless bedroom, lying with the covers pushed away, every breath punctured with a cough.

Nonna couldn't help.

Vittoria went back to the courtyard.

'Fine. All of you, come into the kitchen for a minute. It's all right, you're allowed. Anna-Maria, you're shivering. Are you sick too?'

The girl nodded dumbly. At her side Tonio twisted restlessly.

'My eyes are hot,' Doll complained, pulling at her thin cotton dress. Her arms and legs were covered in a rosy red rash. When she looked down and saw her blistering skin she began to cry, which set Diavolo off too.

'I'll fetch a pen so you can play dot-to-dot drawing,' Vittoria said brightly. Her own skin prickled as she saw something small walk down Doll's sleeve. She dropped to her knees and looked more closely at the children's clothes. The fabric seams were crusted with eggs and lice were crawling everywhere.

'I told you to wash!' she shouted angrily. 'I gave you soap and told you to keep clean except when you were begging! Don't you know what these are? Lice! You're supposed to kill them or they spread disease. I *told* you!'

'We sold the soap,' Diavolo whispered. 'We were hungry.'

She ran upstairs to the salon, where the Contessa was still drinking liqueurs.

'Vittoria! I spoke hastily . . . I didn't mean . . .'

'Never mind that. We need all these cushions. Bring your blankets too . . .'

'I beg your pardon?'

'Come to the kitchen . . . We have to get the oven lit and get some seawater from the marina. The clothes will need boiling.'

'You're raving, child! Slow down and enunciate.'

Enunciate? Fine. Vittoria exaggerated every syllable. 'The children are sick. I think it must be typhus. TY-PHUS. There! Is that clear enough?'

The Contessa was aghast. 'Sick children? Here? Send them to the nurses at the convent.'

'They'll only pray. What good has that ever done anyone?'

'Then send them to the army hospitals. We can't have fever here!'

Vittoria felt like stamping and shouting. There wasn't time for all this fuss. Typhus was a killer. She knew it had flared up in other parts of the city, spread by lice that thrived on dirt and weak people.

'We need medicine.'

'And how do you propose I find the money for that?' The Contessa pressed her handkerchief over her mouth.

Vittoria smiled.

One, two, three, four, five gold coins.

Where was the best place to go first? Via Forcella. She had a contact there. She did what she could for the children in the kitchen then slipped out into the street. It suddenly seemed very hot for autumn, despite the clouds blowing seawards. She shaded her eyes as she hunted through the market stalls, searching for a trader she knew. There he was, rolling dice on a barrel top.

'Paolo, I need medicine.'

'What sort?'

'Any sort.'

'What for? What's wrong?'

'Nothing's wrong. I don't know. Just give me some pills – don't you have any?'

The man Paolo shrugged. 'Just our special home-made remedies.'

'I don't want talc and flour pastilles!' she shouted. 'Fob them off on someone stupid. Have you got proper medicine or not?'

'If you've got proper money.'

She paused. 'I have something to sell . . . Something Roman. Gold.'

'Gold, is it?' Paolo said with a toothless smile. 'Come here and show me, let's see what you've got . . .'

Vittoria tore herself away from his pawing hands. Of course it was too dangerous to barter out in the open like that. How could she be so stupid! Dark faces turned her way, curious and greedy. A squad of British soldiers sauntered along, keeping an eye on things. She quickly dodged round a corner. Where else could she find medicine? A hospital. Which one? What about that photographer woman? The one after the bomb: Margaret Impossible-Name. She'd said she would help. (Would anyone help?) What was the place she mentioned? The 67th Field Hospital, that's what she'd said. Where was it? Why weren't the streets in their proper places any more? Why was the sun so awfully bright?

At the hospital, finally, she stopped for a moment, alarmed by the sight of so many patients. Army nurses were moving around wards and corridors full of stretchers as if dancing a genteel waltz. Wounded and dying lay everywhere. Where had they come from? Not the Post Office explosion, these were soldiers. Of course. The invasion. Fighting, in the mountains. Disgusting. She didn't want to see blood-soaked bandages or gaps where legs should have been. There were some enemy soldiers mixed in with the jumble of Allies. She wondered if Peter Schäfer was one of the broken boys. Hoped he was. Serve him right.

'Where is Bentley-Wyke?' she asked in Italian, wishing

she'd learned English, not German.

Nurse after nurse smiled at Vittoria and none-too-gently shooed her away. 'She's not here,' they said in English, and when Vittoria didn't respond they repeated themselves: 'NOT HERE.'

Not at the hospital? So the stupid English woman couldn't help after all!

Vittoria walked straight into an army doctor.

'What's the rush?' he asked. This she understood because he spoke Italian, though rather fancily, as if reading from a poetry book. 'Are you all right, you poor thing?'

'I'm not a poor thing. I'm fine. Except Bentley-Wyke said she would help and I can't find her.'

'Maggie? The photographer? I know her, she was in here this morning, I haven't seen her since . . .'

Vittoria was already moving away. *Just me*, she thought. *Only ever me. I can do it. I'll find my own medicine. Here's the room. Pick the lock. Too many shelves. Which bottles? Why don't they stop dancing around? Take some. Take all of them. Sell what we don't use . . .*

She left the storeroom and began to walk out of the hospital. The walls weren't very steady. They kept lurching in to brush her arms. There was the main door.

133

The street. The closer she got to it the further away it seemed. That wasn't fair! She started to run. Her feet dragged through treacle. Faster and faster she went until she ran straight into a big green mountain.

It was a man in army uniform, a red-faced sergeant with a matching red cross on his sleeve and a toothpick poking out of the corner of his mouth. He loomed over as if to help but she thought he was after her satchel. Vittoria snatched at it. The strap broke. The bag burst open. Pills and packages scattered everywhere.

There was a woman holding the sergeant's arm. A face she recognised. Margaret Bentley-Wyke.

Vittoria had no idea what the man was yelling, couldn't even stop to untangle Margaret's bad Italian. She had to go. At any moment the Military Police would be upon her. She'd be hauled off to prison and locked up for ever and ever and who'd feed the children and take them medicine and find them safe places to eat and look after them and be their mama and papa and every other living relative and . . .

The sergeant grabbed her.

'I've got money!' she shouted. 'I can pay for these things, I swear. Look, *lira*, take it all, just let me go. You have to let me go! You want more? I have more. A genuine dollar, here . . .'

She hadn't meant to catch hold of the leather pouch. She certainly hadn't wanted it to fall open. The sergeant gawped at the five gold coins tumbling to the ground. She bit his hand, tasted blood, caught up four of the coins and ran.

Wandering Minds

November was a tad early for New Year's Resolutions but one of the things I decided was not to be so *predictable*. It was something to do with seeing all those black coats at the Remembrance Service and Dr Shepherd's bright colours. Not that I went out and bought look-at-me neon gear. I was just sick of everything trudging on and on and on in exactly the same way. Craig had his cross-country running. I had . . . zilch. The internet was down, there was nothing on TV and homework was, miraculously, done. Time to get less *grey*.

I didn't know precisely what I'd say when I went round to number sixty-four. The nice thing was, I didn't have to say anything. Dr Shepherd just opened the door and smiled.

'Hello, come in, I think you will like some chocolate cake.'

She covered the old skull with a tea towel and we sat down at the kitchen table. I sat with my back to the eight shiny bullets. Jazz music was playing in the next room and I heard Mr Shepherd humming along. The cake was good, home-made, not one of the boring supermarket ones. I turned down a second slice.

'I'll get fat.'

'Stupidity! You have to eat. Food is good. Be active, that is all. I walk every day but it gets so cold in this country, then I walk somewhere anyway but I get to a street and cannot remember where I am. Idiot! Fortunately, Winnie always knows the way home. Always we have a dog with us called Winnie. When this lady is gone I don't know how I will manage.' The little dog was sleeping on a cushion under the table, next to the radiator. She gave a hoarse bark.

My heart started beating fast. I suddenly knew why I'd come – to do a favour.

'You said Winnie was going into kennels while your husband's in hospital. What if she didn't have to? Me and Craig could look after her, couldn't we? We'd be dead careful and let her dig in the garden as much as she likes. Can we do that?'

Her face! I'd never noticed how *deep* her eyes were. I was looking right into another human being. It was embarrassing to see so many emotions there. I felt my cheeks go hot so I dived into another bit of cake. Most people would've said, 'No no it doesn't matter, we'll manage.' Dr Shepherd didn't mess about like that.

'You will look after Winnie? That is *very* kind and makes me happy.' She lowered her voice. 'This Winnie has been with us for fifteen years. My husband was so worried about leaving her in a strange place.'

'We'll keep an eye on the house too, if you're away long.'

She stretched out a bony hand and patted my arm. 'I knew you would help. I meant to do everything myself, but there is no time. And here you are! Young and healthy and ready to go. You will pay for nothing. All will be provided. I know a good hotel in Naples. Hotel Sanfelice. Once it was an elegant home, a Contessa lived there, now you can stay, I will arrange for rooms. The trains are easy. Even without Mussolini they run on time.'

Whoa! Hold up there! Pause! Replay! At what point did I say anything about hotels in Naples? Dr Shepherd never noticed I went into panic mode. Her eyes had shifted to another place.

'You will go in August when it is very hot. Be careful. Stay inside during the afternoon and wear a hat. Much nicer than going in winter. It can be cold, even in the south of Italy. The mountains are worst. Snow and ice everywhere. But in August it is wonderfully sunny. When you go to see the man, it must be in the dark – no arguments – night-time! On the beach. I'll draw a map. And don't stay too long – it is dangerous, you understand? Make sure you escape afterwards. What else? Crime of course, that is bad, and yes, the volcano exists. Vesuvius is quiet, quiet for now, no steam even. Will it erupt again? Maybe yes, maybe no. The last time was 1944, you know. A terrible time, after a terrible winter. So many people died – the hunger, the fever, the fighting too.'

Suddenly *boring* didn't seem such a bad thing. I couldn't stop her talking, couldn't even bring myself to get up and go.

'Fever?'

'Vittoria was ill. They were all ill. The Contessa was so bad she couldn't prevent the orphans sheltering in her house. Eight of them there were, that winter. Vittoria took care of them all. There should have been nine, but one boy died, yes, died, and there was nothing to do about it. His sister was broken-hearted. Vittoria stole some flowers for the grave. There was no headstone. They didn't even know the little boy's name to write on one. They didn't pray either, not even Nina Dragone, who went to church every Sunday when the bakery was closed. Such a good girl, and look what happened to her after the war!'

'Wait up, you said a boy *died*? Didn't, like, the authorities do anything?'

'What could they do? Hundreds of people sick with disease and too thin to fight the fever! In some parts of the city they dusted everyone with DDT, big clouds of chemicals, to make them better.' She mimed the actions of a pump spray. 'That was the army, helping. The rest of the soldiers were fighting to push the Germans out of Italy. Every little inch, they fought. Capture one mountain . . . find more Germans waiting for them on the next! Then they came to Monte Cassino. Oh that slowed the Allies down all right. Months they were there, fighting for that mountain. The valley around the mountain was the only way to get to Rome, you see, so the Germans were going to defend it to the last man. And it almost was the last man, believe me.'

'Maybe you shouldn't worry about all this now.'

'Worry? Who is worried? What are you worried about? Your brother, is that it? He will be fine. They are tough, paratroopers. Now let me see, what else? There was another soldier, the one with the sword on Herculaneum beach, August the twenty-fourth. The day the volcano exploded. Or was it March? *Non ricordo bene*. Before the volcano, Vittoria saw him. No, during the volcano. How could she tell what she saw when she had fever and hunger? At that time in the war everyone was a little strange in the head. Look, you should get ready or it will be too late! What time is it? I have to pack. Time goes so quickly and it will be August again too soon! Where is my bag? Was it stolen? The gold was stolen.'

Oh this was bonkers! 'You *gave* us the gold coin. I'll go fetch it back if you like.'

'No, no, that one is for you. For helping. *Can you help?*'

She pushed back her chair and stood up. She obviously had no clue what to do next so she glared at me. Was I supposed to fetch her husband, or sun cream for summer in Naples? Under the table Winnie licked my shoes. I tried suggesting Dr Shepherd should just take it easy for a minute. That didn't go down well.

'A minute? One minute, two minutes, hours, days, years. *Tempus fugit*, that's what I taught at the university. *Time flies.* You know that once I lectured in Classics at Cambridge? All those Latin writers, and as a girl I made ridicule of them. So long ago and almost yesterday. Time flies like an eagle. Like an aeroplane. I never flew. I hate the sound of the engines just before the bombs drop. Your passport is valid? Craig also?'

Yes, actually, but that was hardly the point.

141

She began to turn in circles round the room. 'Things hide from me . . . People disappear. We could ask Margaret, she knows how to find people. She found Vittoria's papa . . . but that was after the war, when they opened Auschwitz and found the bodies but all the rats had run away . . .'

It was horrible, seeing her rummage in the kitchen cupboards, almost shaking with anxiety because she couldn't find her passport. Then she came across the crumpled newspaper parcel we'd seen the very first day we came over. I watched her carry everything to the table with exaggerated care. She stroked the green wool insignia and brushed her fingers over the other objects. She seemed to grow smaller.

I slipped through the plastic curtain to the lounge, where Mr Shepherd was still listening to jazz. He struggled to his feet when I said maybe he should come and look after his wife. It was sweet, seeing him talk to her till she was calm again.

'Is she all right?'

She heard me whispering and smiled at both of us.

'Me? I'm fine, of course! What was I saying? I forget. Never mind! Shall I put the kettle on? So kind of you to take Winnie, so very kind. Your mother will not object?'

What could I say except reassure her?

'Mum's working a lot. She won't mind, really.' (Roughly translated as: she'll blow her top but it'll be too late by then.) Anyway, I thought, who cares about Mum, she's never in anyway so why shouldn't we have Winnie to keep us company? Not that I'm mad at Mum for working, she has to, she's a single parent. I wondered if I should get a job and help out, then I'd have more money and I could go out more, go on dates, go out with Gavin Parker . . .

All connection between brain and mouth being severed I suddenly blurted out, 'There's a boy I like. He asked me out once and I blew it. Fat chance he'll ask me again.'

'That is easy,' Dr Shepherd answered. 'You ask him.'

'*Me* ask *him* out?'

Mr Shepherd nodded agreement. (Great. I was getting dating advice from geriatrics.) He said, 'Why not? *Audaces fortuna iuvat*. Fortune favours . . .'

'. . . the bold. Yeah. I guess.'

No more mention of Naples or Monte Cassino. Instead I went home and had Mum struggling to decide whether I was an angel or daughter from hell, for offering to dog-sit. Craig went all gooey at the thought of having a pet, even just a temporary one. It was pretty nice in the end and everything worked out fine. Winnie made a great hot-water bottle on the nights when I sneaked her up to my bedroom, just like that dog Craig was on about, who

143

kept Peter and Erich warm in the mountains.

One day Mum came back from work and cooked us all a massive vat of spag bol. She said she'd looked in on Mr Shepherd at the hospital.

'Is he going to be OK?' I asked.

'That's what they're testing him to find out. He's a nice man when you talk to him. He loves his jazz music. I think that's what's keeping him going, wanting to play again. That and looking after his wife.'

Craig shook his head. 'She looks after him. He's poorly a lot.'

'She's not well either, Craig. I've seen her at the hospital a few times and she's been very sweet, much nicer than I first thought, but I've noticed the deterioration in her speech even after a couple of conversations. Poor lady. She hates getting muddled. It must be awful to see your memories disappear one by one. Dementia is a terrible condition.'

Dementia. The disease that eats your memory bit by bit . . .

Time is running out.

I lost my appetite for spaghetti. It started snowing. I didn't care. Believe it or not, I actually went hunting for my passport after tea. Rich made us all get valid ones so we could travel places, only we never did. God knows why I dug it up that evening. The old lady's worries were nothing to do with me, right? So why was I spending hours staring at the gold coin wondering whether Dr Shepherd would ever be lucid enough to tell me what was so urgent?

She'd asked me, *Can you help?*

What did she need me to do?

Christmas Letters

Dear All

It's snow-tastic out here! A tad nippy so we're breaking out the long johns. Wish u could see the mountains. They're pretty impressive. Too rocky 4 skiing. Good to hear you're all well. I'm fine. Stumpy's got a cold, which he reckons is flu. Wuss.

It was great your letters found me cos we've been moving around a lot. All in a good cause. Now we're making the area safe, the locals are starting to chill out a bit, some come n say hello. They reckon there might be proper democratic elections soon, which'll be a miracle. Can't imagine people getting so excited about the chance to vote back home. There's even talk of a school opening and the local kids are keen on that, specially the girls who haven't had the chance to go before.

I'll write proper letters to u, D & C, promise. F.Y.I, Craig, yeah I have heard of Monte Cassino it was a real hell for both sides. *The German paras were class. Fought like devils but always stopped so wounded could get sorted. Haven't heard of Peter Schäfer. It wasn't like just one or two men were heroes, they all were.*

Anyway, could u say thanks to Mr & Mrs Shepherd, can't believe they packed a Chrimbo parcel for us lads - stars. We troughed all the cakes n Italian biscuits straight off n had an early Xmas party with the rest of the grub they sent, it was like a night out at Antonio's – salami n ham n cheeses. Tell them thanks for the 'Silver Eagles' CD, it got us well jazzed up. Hadn't heard of that band before. It rocks.

Not going to manage much 4 u guys this Xmas, I'm dead jealous you'll be opening pressies without me. We get Xmas dinner here. Me n Stumpy are in charge of decorating the mess tent so it'll look like the dog's b-ll-cks or the dog's dinner, depending how much beer we have first. Only kidding, Mum! We're all good boys . . . !

This letter's longer than a bog roll. Gotta go now.

Ho! Ho! Ho! Have a good one!

Luv Rich xx

Two whole kisses to share out between us.

Only Mr Shepherd was in when me and Craig went over to show him Rich's letter. I asked if Dr Shepherd was out

Christmas shopping for him.

'I'll be lucky to get some new socks!' he snorted, but his eyes were twinkly. If the parcel they'd sent to Rich was anything to go by, I bet they had a right old nosh-up at Christmas. I already knew from Dr Shepherd that she was planning to take her hubby out to Antonio's restaurant as a festive treat.

He liked the letter.

'It's good you keep writing,' he said. 'Soldiers are away so long, they worry about people back home.'

Craig asked, 'Did Peter Schäfer get letters?'

Mr Shepherd sort of shrugged. 'Yes. Yes, his family wrote to him. It wasn't always the best news. His first Christmas away he heard his father was taken into the army even though he was just a farmer. By 1944 British and American bombers were easily targeting German cities. Josef Goebbels, Hitler's Minister for Propaganda, he still preached ultimate Nazi victory. The newspapers didn't give proper details of all the defeats in Russia and Italy. Mind you, the German army held fast at Monte Cassino, much longer than anyone expected.'

His voice dwindled. I suddenly noticed how old he was. He hadn't been the same since that stint in hospital. Then he revived. 'Did you know the monastery at Monte Cassino is the most bombed building in the history of warfare?'

'That's daft,' Craig said. 'Why bomb a monastery? Don't they just have, like, monks there?'

Turns out the monastery was on top of a mountain and had a brilliant viewpoint over this place called the Liri Valley. The road to Rome ran through this valley and the Allies had to get to Rome.

Mr Shepherd said, 'One man with a pair of binoculars and a radio could communicate the slightest movement in the valley, which meant artillery fire could be targeted and accurate. How could the Allies liberate Rome if they couldn't get past the defences in that valley? Some said the Germans had troops in the monastery. Some said even the Germans would respect its ancient heritage and keep the monastery out of the war. All just words. The vantage point had to be neutralised. You can't imagine how it was. On February fifteenth 1944, the first clear day for weeks, wave after wave of planes passed over Monastery Hill, just as the monks were kneeling for morning prayer. Hundreds of tons of explosives were dropped followed by hour after hour of artillery. It didn't seem possible that anyone could survive such destruction.'

I shivered and thought of the green *Fallschirmjäger* insignia Dr Shepherd had shown us. Perhaps that was the day Peter Schäfer died.

The Truce

February 1944

Peter jerked out of an uneasy doze thinking, *Mum! It's too early for school!*

Someone rough and dirty was shaking him awake. 'Our turn for lookout, Turnip.'

Erich. Oh God. This was not his bed at home but a bitterly cold hole crammed full of men and kit. This was still Monte Cassino.

Paper crackled as he shifted to leave the dugout that had been his home for the past week. He'd actually drifted off in the middle of reading new letters from home. There must have been a precious lull in the sound of artillery explosions splintering round the valley. Sleep had to be stolen whenever possible.

Crouching low he picked his way across the rocky shelter, jostling friends and empty food cans. He was layered in every bit of clothing he owned, all of it stained. He pulled a grubby woollen scarf over his head, wincing as it rubbed all the scabs on his scalp from trying to shave with a blunt razor. Mittens covered his cracked hands but not the split nails.

'Do me a favour – leave the door open and let some heat in!' Jupp said softly.

Erich grinned. 'If you'd be kind enough to stop hogging the bathroom and using up all the hot water, dear boy.'

There was no door, no bathroom, and no water, hot or cold. They washed, rarely, in melted snow.

Peter eased out of the shelter after Erich, glad the moon was shrouded. The huge mass of the mountain was invisible but eerily present. By day they'd see the wide spread of the valley below and the gimlet windows of the great monastery above. By day they'd be spotted by enemy troops and shot for certain.

They'd learned to be creatures of the night.

He crawled forward to a low wall of bulging sandbags. Here an MG42 machine gun nestled darkly. He could strip and reassemble it blindfold. Fire it without hesitating. Change the barrel in seconds when it overheated.

Next to the weapon were two camouflaged bodies that shifted to make room.

'About time you came to relieve us,' murmured Heini Holz. He and Lanky wasted no time heading back to the shelter.

Nestling down by the machine gun Erich suddenly asked, 'What date is it?'

Peter had to think. 'February thirteenth, no, it's just after midnight, so February the fourteenth. What's that snort for?'

'Much good Valentine's Day will do us here in this pit. My lips are too chapped for smooching and my hands are too damned cold for feeling girls up, even if there were any for miles around.'

'Stick your hands in your armpits to keep them warm.'

'I'd rather stick them up Lily Marlene's sweater. I suppose Winston the hot-water bottle will have to do instead. At least you've got the lovely Lisa to dream about.'

Peter lay down flat and became part of the rocky mountainside.

'The lovely Lisa, as you call her, has . . . has written to call the whole thing off. That was one of the letters I got.'

'Hey, I'm sorry . . .'

Even though he was furious, Peter kept his anger barely audible. Sound travelled at night. No telling who was listening.

'*You've never been to see me*, she says, *and your letters are very short*. What does the stupid girl expect? How can men be spared for a week's leave when the Allies just keep sending more troops at us? And where am I supposed to get paper from on this barren mountainside? There's nothing to write on and next to nothing to read. I'm sick of reading the ration packet labels then using them for bum-fodder.'

He felt Erich's fist on his arm – a friendly punch. 'You're better off without her, you know that.'

Peter didn't reply. *You don't love me*, Lisa had written. He honestly couldn't argue with that. For all Erich's banter about Valentine's Day, love was part of a different world. All Peter knew was that he'd trained and fought at the side of the men in the dugout. He lived for them. He'd die for them.

'The letter from Mother was pretty normal,' he said eventually. 'She wants to know if we've won yet.'

'Tell her we will.'

Peter nodded in the dark. *We will. We'd better.*

Something moved on the mountainside, beyond the dugout. Instantly he was alert. Friend or foe? He looked for the shape of a helmet. Hissed a challenge. No reply. Called again. Nothing. He narrowed his eyes against muzzle flare and fired off a few rounds from the machine gun, proud to hear he'd hit his target straight away, then confused as an awful *haw-he-haw-he-haw* noise filled the night.

Erich stuffed a mitten in his mouth to choke down laughter. Tears ran down his cold cheeks.

'My God, Turnip, you've killed a donkey,' he whispered as soon as he could talk. 'What a hero of the Fatherland! That deserves the iron cross and a handshake from Hitler at the very least!'

Darkness hid Peter's flaming cheeks. One of the supply mules! He'd never live this down! There'd be endless sniggering he-haws from the lads. *Stop making that damned row!* he thought, as the mule kept braying desperately. He fired off another round. Silence for a few seconds . . . until he heard the familiar brief hiss that meant a mortar was about to land. The night exploded with dazzling lights and hideous noises. As expected, here was the next bombardment. Nothing intense, just business as usual for Monastery Hill.

Over the noise of the artillery fire Erich kindly recited the *Fallschirmjäger* fifth commandment: 'Remember, dear Turnip, *The most precious thing in the presence of the foe is ammunition. He who shoots uselessly, merely to comfort himself, is a man of straw who merits not the title of parachutist.'* He wiggled back to the dugout to catch a few hours' rest underground. 'As for the donkey, well – schoolboy error.'

Peter's blood ran as cold as the snow. *Does he know?* It had been a long time since he thought about school.

He shredded Lisa's letter and stuffed it in his boots for extra insulation. Time to watch for enemy troops advancing under cover of the artillery. No time to worry about letters, about girls, about anything other than doing his job.

Another watch ended. Morning came – a morning that tasted of explosives. When a message arrived to say there would be a two-hour truce at eight a.m., to collect wounded and bury the dead, he volunteered to act as stretcher-bearer. Erich, Jupp and another para called Max came too. It was a great novelty to be able to go out in the weak sunshine. Their Italian suntans had long since faded.

Winston trotted on ahead as they worked their way round and down the mountain flank. Habit made them run with hunched shoulders and heads low.

'That b——d monastery,' swore Erich, looking up. 'Doesn't matter which way you go, where you hide, it's always there, watching. I hate it, *hate* it.'

Peter nodded. It was true, like the eyes of a painting in a haunted house, there was no escaping the gaze of the monastery's blank windows. It seemed indifferent to the marks of war that scarred both the mountain and the valley.

'Over here!'

One voice soon became a chorus of, 'Medic! Medic!'

Peter lost track of how many bloodied men they carried back to the rough aid station. Then he stumbled into a soldier with strips of his face hanging off and a bright clot of blood where his neck should've been.

He stopped short and asked, 'What about corpses? The ground's too hard to bury them.'

'Cover them with rocks,' was the only reply.

He bent down, then jumped back in shock as the dead man moved and tried to speak, but that only made blood gurgle from the wound. Worse, he wasn't speaking German, but English.

'A Yank, still alive,' said Erich, prodding the man's shoulder stripes. 'Get the others over here with the stretcher. We'll get him down to the Allied Red Cross.'

Peter stared at the man's face. It was the closest he'd ever been to the enemy. All his targets had been from a distance before. He'd never had to watch the light disappear from someone's eyes.

'I thought . . . I thought they'd look more evil,' he said as they scrambled down the rocky slope with the stretcher, one man on each pole. He eyed the cluster of enemy soldiers under a limp Red Cross flag. The paratroopers were clear about honouring truces to see to fallen comrades. Would the Allies be the same?

They lowered the stretcher and turned to go.

'Wait.'

Peter froze. A British medic was talking to them – a big brute of a sergeant with red hair and a toothpick twirling in the corner of his mouth. 'Thanks,' the man said. '*Danke*. Speak English?'

Jupp muttered, 'Do I bullocks,' in German. Peter knew how to say, *Hello, Goodbye* and *How about a nice cup of tea?* So he did.

The sergeant's face cracked into a smile and all the nearby soldiers laughed.

'D'you hear that?' he bellowed. '*Hello, goodbye, how about a nice mucking cup of tea*? Reckon we could all do with one of them, eh? Get a bloody bit of warmth in our bellies. I haven't been toasty since we took Naples and I met this nice lady journalist. Here, fancy a smoke, Fritz?'

'Peter, not Fritz.'

That made the sergeant laugh even more. 'Peter, not

Fritz, he says. I like it! Fritz is just a name for you Jerries, see? Like you call us Brits Tommies, and you can call the Yanks what you like! I'm Joe. Joe Sharpe. Royal Sussex Regiment and proud of it. We're giving you blokes a bit of a knocking, right? Why don't you just quit and let us get on our way to Rome, save everyone some bother? Saying that, you paras fight ruddy well considering you're fascist scum. Where're you from?'

Only Erich could understand the rapid-fire words.

'I'm from Berlin,' he said, then switched to English. 'A beautiful city before you British bombed it.'

'Yeah? When we win the war I fancy visiting Adolf's house in Berlin to say, *Hello, goodbye, how about a nice cup of tea and here's my gun in your gob for all the bombs you dropped on us, mate*. Oh don't get shirty. I'm just having a laugh, aren't I? Way I see it, we're all in this stink together. Me, I'm a butcher by trade, had a cushy little job in Eastbourne, so what did they do when I signed up for this lark? Made me a mucking medic, that's what. Army logic for you. Still, I mean to get what I can out of the war, if you know what I mean.'

Here the sergeant produced a gold coin, as if from thin air. He twirled it in his fingers.

'Lovely, innit? Proper antique too – original Roman. Reckon I know where I can get me some more, too, once

I track down the *signorina* who loaned me this one . . .'

He tossed the coin high in the air, caught it, closed his fist round it then slapped it, unseen, on to the back of his grimy hand.

'Heads we win the war, tails you don't, ha ha!'

When Sharpe revealed the coin Peter saw the round face of a Roman emperor looking up at him.

'That's Vespasian,' he said. 'He started building the Colosseum.'

Sergeant Sharpe picked out one word from the German. 'The Colosseum? I fancy seeing that when we get to Rome.'

Erich threw his cigarette stub into the dirty snow. 'You'll have to get past us first.'

The sergeant kept on working as he talked, even though his face was haggard with exhaustion. Like an automaton he tore open bloodied uniforms, injected morphine and scattered powder on open wounds. An unlikely hero, Peter thought, but a kind of hero all the same.

'Me 'n' me dad,' Sharpe continued, 'we almost took a trip to Deutschland back in '36 when they had the Olympics.'

Peter smiled at that last word. The Olympics! That brought back a whole summer of sweet memories, hearing radio reports of Olympic torch runners racing across every country between Athens and Berlin, collecting magazine pictures for his scrapbook . . .

Germany had won the most gold medals of course. Thirty-three, compared to Britain's measly four.

He accepted a British cigarette. Erich leaned in to light it for him and murmured, in German, 'I lived near the Olympic village. I used to wait hours to get autographs from the athletes.'

'I was going to train for the Olympics if I hadn't signed up for this.'

'D'you remember when Jesse Owens got his fourth gold medal? He was a god!'

Without thinking Peter replied, 'Yeah, I remember, even though I was only seven. No, not seven. I must've been older. Nine. Definitely nine. Ten even.'

Erich gave him a long, hard stare.

Sharpe was oblivious to Peter's blunder. 'Jesse Owens, you say? He ran like muck off a shovel. Four gold medals in one Olympics! Put old Adolf's nose right out of joint to have a black chap win over all you blond superheroes.'

There was a collective shrug and more cigarette smoking. Photos of wives, families and girlfriends were shown. Jupp fished out his battered Leica camera to take pictures of himself wearing a British forage cap and posing with a Lee Enfield rifle. Max let one of the Americans admire his unauthorised Luger pistol . . . from a distance.

Peter checked his watch. Almost ten o'clock. The truce was trickling to an end. This wasn't half-time at a soccer match, this was a lull in the slaughter. So be it. He glanced over at the American they'd rescued, who was frothing up one last flood of blood. No last words for him. No words at all, just death.

'Waste of effort carrying him down there,' Lanky complained as they trudged back to their dugout with the stained stretcher.

'*Auf Wiedersehen*, you devils,' Sergeant Sharpe shouted. 'God Save the King!'

'I'll give him my regards when we conquer London,' Erich called. 'Is Princess Elizabeth still single?'

Peter stayed back a little and spoke to Erich in private. 'About what I said . . . about being only seven in '36 . . . did Max or Jupp hear?'

'Ears full of wax. But just remember not everyone is as lousy at adding as those two.'

Later in the day American planes appeared in the pale blue sky, above the range of German anti-aircraft guns. A cluster of white objects began to fall, too big to be snow, too gentle to be bombs. They were sheets of paper, hundreds and hundreds of them, falling round the monastery and the mountain slopes. Peter caught one and smoothed it flat, thinking, *At last there's something new to read.* It was in English, so he couldn't understand it. Another sheet fell nearby, this time in Italian. He struggled to pick meaning from the typewritten sentences. It said:

Italian friends,

BEWARE!

We have until now been especially careful to avoid shelling the Monte Cassino Monastery. The Germans have known how to benefit from this. But now the fighting has swept closer and closer to its sacred precincts. The time has come when we must train our guns on the monastery itself.

We give you warning so that you may save yourselves. We warn you urgently: leave the monastery. Leave it at once. Respect this warning. It is for your benefit.

THE US FIFTH ARMY

The next morning three waves of American planes filled the skies. Bombs fell, endlessly it seemed, worse than any of the usual bombardments. Ears ringing and head pounding, Peter crouched in the crevice dugout next to Erich. He felt like a tiny ant under giant footfalls. Rocks shattered and the roof caved in. He risked a quick glance up and in that one second saw smoke coiling as high as the heavens, and flames flaring from the monastery ruins. Yet another bomb fell.

The mountain burned.

Ruins

February 1944

I'm not dead. This was Peter's first thought. Then, *Where's Erich?*

'Hey, Turnip. . .'

The familiar voice was muted by the ringing in Peter's ears.

Shaking after the last bomb fell and the last evil echo ricocheted round the valley, the platoon crawled out into a deformed landscape. High above, a jagged outline could just be glimpsed through thick black smoke. Peter rubbed his eyes, which were streaming in the gritty air. How could a single stone of the monastery be left after such an onslaught? Four walls still stood, though jagged and cracked. Giant blocks of masonry had tumbled down the mountainside.

Orders came to scramble for cover in the monastery ruins. Peter somehow willed his legs to move. He looked up as they went through the monastery entrance and almost laughed. There was one word painted in bold red above the door. PAX. The Latin for Peace.

Not much else was intact. They moved carefully through the mounds of debris, past columns snapped into stumps and choir stalls blasted into a sharp mass of splinters. A charred wooden cross tilted over a cairn of medieval rubble. A saint's statue had been decapitated and speckled with shrapnel cuts.

Peter couldn't help remembering the lieutenant-colonel back at Vittoria's house in Naples, the one who said treasures from Pompeii and Herculaneum would be stored at the monastery. He hoped the rumours were true – that all valuables had been moved to Rome before the war came to Cassino.

Mahler, now promoted to a sergeant, warned, 'Keep an eye out for unexploded shells and search for survivors. Let me know if you spot a monk under all this mess. I've always wanted to see one in the flesh. Look lively, lads. This Allied tea-break won't last for ever.'

There was no time to rest. Peter and Erich worked side by side, digging where they could, using bare hands and rifle butts to get to the source of screams and moans. They found few survivors and lots of bodies, including women and children.

'Refugees,' Mahler said grimly. 'About a hundred turned up here in a storm one night, hysterical with fear. Wouldn't leave, whatever the monks said. Too late now.'

Stopping for a fierce gulp of schnapps, Peter was amazed to see a man lurching across the rubble to bring Holy Sacrament to a group of monks who were determined to celebrate communion at the correct hour, without interruption.

Once he looked up and thought he saw another plane, but it was an eagle, an honest-to-God golden eagle, soaring in the air as if there was no such thing as war.

Later he came across a boy about his sister Sophie's age, crushed under a chunk of yellow-veined marble. The boy was bleeding from his tear ducts. His last words were, 'Mama, Mama!'

Erich pulled Peter away. 'Leave him. Nothing you can do. Give me a hand with this old granny. We're going to carry her out on a ladder then we're ordered down to defend Cassino. The Allies'll probably move in after dark, thinking we're all flattened after that bomb frenzy. Moonrise at oh-two-hundred hours. You wait.'

The Abbot of Monte Cassino gathered all civilian survivors under the sign of PAX. The whole bedraggled procession began to stumble down the mountain away from the massing Allied forces. German soldiers from another division moved into the shadow of the monastery walls at nightfall. Good luck to them all, Peter thought. And good luck to us, defending Cassino against whatever the Allies want to throw at us.

They were in earshot of the first enemy assault. He heard explosions first then screams as Allied infantry moved forward into thorny bushes laced with mines, or got tangled on tripwire. The air flashed with human fireworks each time a new explosion was triggered. He'd set some of those booby-traps himself – textbook defence tactics. Now he sicked up a stomach full of nothing.

He thought of his toy soldiers, who stood up again after every mock battle and every dramatic death. Only one had been killed for real, when his sister Sophie threw it into the fire. The paint had burned first, then the metal melted and the soldier became a formless puddle of lead. That was exactly how he felt now. As tired as a legion of sleepwalkers. Only the shadowy presence of Erich at his side kept him stumbling towards their new position.

This isn't how it's meant to be, said a little voice in his mind.

What about the Ultimate Victory Hitler and Goebbels had always promised them? He suddenly thought of the girl in Naples – Victory . . . Vittoria . . . In This Sign Victorious. What had she said back at the café? *Protect yourselves*, that's what she hissed. He thought he *was* protected. He had eagles on his lapel. A golden eagle had flown over him earlier, all those hours-felt-like-centuries ago. That was a lucky sign, surely.

But he felt so small! Had Erich noticed? Somehow his legs kept moving and his shoulder bent under the weight of the machine gun. *Don't want to play any more! Let's stop and everyone, get up and go in for lemonade*. . .Were they going to die? Really die and not get up again?

He thought of that British medic, Sergeant Sharpe, with his twirling gold coin. Vespasian. Hadn't Vespasian refused to die lying down? Prof Meyer had once mentioned the emperor's last joke: 'Oh dear, I think I'm becoming a god.' *Who came after Vespasian? Titus, that's the one.* Titus was in charge when the volcano blew. Titus made the deathbed declaration, 'I have only done one thing wrong.' What was that wrong thing? *Damned if I know. When I'm dead I'll go and ask him.*

But not yet. Don't want to die yet . . .

What would his Last Words to Erich be? Could he manage something Latin to suit the Roman land he'd die in?

Iam me tempus alio vocat; tu valebis!

Not that Erich would understand Latin, of course. Better stick to German – *It's time for me to go now, farewell!*

Better still, not die at all.

If only he could just sleep for a while . . . for a week.

The rocky descent seemed to go on for ever. Behind him the monastery still smouldered. In the distance another mountain burned with faint flickers of fire, far away from the slopes of Monte Cassino.

Vesuvius was getting restless.

Cheating

Two heads are better than one, that's what they say, right? Sadly, one of the heads was Craig's, so I'm not sure the saying holds true. All the same, I didn't know who else to ask. I've hardly got close friends at school. The ones I do hang out with would run a mile if I started going on about the war, any war. If they didn't start spouting *baby-killing-butcher-of-Basra* tosh, they'd be, like, what's that got to do with us? I totally understand. War only happens to other people, in other places, right? Well now I wanted to know too: *what's it got to do with me?*

One afternoon I told Tariq to get stuffed and badgered Craig on the way home.

'She's obviously got a bee in her bonnet about something that needs doing, or something we need to do, only she's got a screw loose – a toolbox of them loose –

and I can't make sense of anything she says now.'

'Who?'

'Dr Shepherd, dummy.'

'She always sounds fine to me. We talk about Richard and paratroopers.'

'What about the other soldier?'

'What other soldier?'

'The one with the sword that Vittoria met on Herculaneum beach.'

He frowned. 'She never said anything about . . . oh, you mean Justinius? He was a Roman legionary. They were amazing fighters, really disciplined. Did you know—'

'Sock in it. Look, it can't be the same guy Vittoria knew during the war cos Justinius is the one the gold money came from.'

'Makes sense. Roman money from a Roman soldier.'

'Oh come on – you can't seriously believe all that. How can we even tell if *anything* she's on about is true? Why'm I even bothering about it?'

He grinned. 'I know what we can do.'

'What?'

'Cheat!'

Easier said than done. It took ages for the computer at home to crank up and get a connection, then Craig was a pain in the bum arguing who'd get the swivel chair, so we decided to flip a coin (not the gold one) and it fell down a gap in the floorboards (proving it's a good idea to have carpets in all rooms) so he grabbed the chair off me and it collapsed when the back fell off. Problem solved. We both knelt on the floor.

I got hold of the keyboard and typed *Herculaneum soldier* into the search engine, thinking there'd be zero results. Wrong. According to the squillion sites that came up, there really was a soldier from Herculaneum. There was also a twist. The very first link I clicked on showed a photo of a brown, mottled skeleton lying face down, bone arms stretched over its head. Very dead.

'There's the sword on his right side,' said Craig. 'Still in a scabbard. Cool.'

I skimmed the text. Skeleton of Roman man uncovered by accident way back in the Eighties when modern workmen were sorting out drainage problems at Herculaneum. Remains of a Roman lady found not far away, with two gold rings on her skeleton fingers. In twelve big arcades close by hundreds more skeletons (hideous pictures) including lots of children – all distorted in agony. They'd all died in AD79, when Vesuvius erupted.

I heard a little voice in my mind, a grey man whispering: *Can you help?* Heard it. Ignored it. Enough loons around with Dr Fruitloop next door.

I read off the screen, '*The pyroclastic blast was so strong it forced the soldier to the ground and broke every bone in his body apart from one in his ear.*'

'Wicked.'

'*Archaeologists examined the remains and discovered he was about thirty-seven years old, with marks on his bones to suggest he'd done a lot of hard riding. He may have been a cavalry soldier. He had an old wound on his left leg which would have caused a limp. Facial reconstruction . . .*'

'What's that?'

'When they fake up a face to see what he would've looked like. This guy obviously had a whopping big nose. *Three teeth are missing from his front jaw, possibly lost in a fight.* Blah blah blah, more bone stuff . . . Here we go: *Like most Roman soldiers he also practised a trade. He carried a bag of carpentry tools on his back, possibly snatched up as Vesuvius erupted. At his waist a leather pouch was found containing . . .* Oh my God.'

'What?'

'Look.'

I scrolled down. There on the screen was a photograph showing bright round shapes stuck in a dark mass. Gold Roman coins.

After that we went a bit mad searching for info.

The name *Peter Schäfer* didn't turn up any relevant hits.

Neither did *Vittoria Venafro*. There were thousands of pages about Vesuvius, including the revelation that it last erupted in March 1944, so Dr Shepherd had been right about that.

'After the truce,' Craig said.

'What truce?'

'Remember Mr Shepherd said the Germans and Allies kept having truces so they could get their wounded and bury the dead.'

'Even though they'd just been murdering the hell out of each other?'

'It's sort of a rule of war. There was a truce on Valentine's Day, before the Allies bombed the monastery of Monte Cassino to pieces.'

He made appropriate explosion noises. Boys are born with a genetic necessity to do that, along with a tendency to pick up any long thin object to fire as a weapon making pathetic bang-bang gunshot sounds. However, my ears perked up at the name *Monte Cassino*, since that was another place Dr Shepherd had mentioned. If I could just put all the pieces into places there might even be a pattern, something that made sense.

We had a collective moment of genius and looked up a map of the area. There was Rome. Across from Rome, sort of right and down a bit, was the town of Cassino. We switched to a satellite view and zoomed in.

'Well that's dud,' I said. 'There's the monastery right there, on top of the zigzag road up the mountain.'

'Cool.'

'*Not* cool! How can it be there when Mr Shepherd says it was bombed to smithereens?'

'They rebuilt it, obviously.'

I stared at my brother. Since when did he get so knowledgeable? Freaky.

Naples was south of Rome on the coast. You couldn't miss nearby Vesuvius – it was a big brown wilderness on the satellite image with a whopping wide-open crater.

I typed in *Naples World War 2*. We had to trawl through a load of blah then we got a shock. Up popped the very same photo Dr Shepherd had shown us on Remembrance Sunday, only this one wasn't creased of course. It was definitely the same shot of the girl covered head-to-toe in grey dust with a streak of dark blood down one side of her face. The caption read, *The True Face of War, 20th October 1943 – Naples Post Office Bomb. Margaret Bentley-Wyke.*

Margaret. Why did that name sound familiar? Hadn't Dr Shepherd mentioned her? Was she the girl in the photo or the person who took it? It had to be weird, taking pictures of war. Wouldn't you just want to put the camera down and, I don't know, help out? Or maybe you have to leave first-aid stuff to proper nurses and doctors so you can do your job showing people what war looks like. I wondered if Rich would be on TV, out in Afghanistan.

Craig was poking the keyboard to misspell *Fallschirmjäger Italy World War 2*.

I said, 'Stuff that boring boy stuff.'

Craig went right on scrolling through pictures of lads in German uniform. It was true some of them looked really young, but they weren't soft or scared. Maybe it was all bluff. When Craig was really little he used to go around saying he'd punch any dinosaur that tried to eat him. That's what the boys at school are like too, macho on the outside, marshmallows inside. (Was Gary Parker like that too? I still hadn't made a move on him, and he was just, you know, regular friendly with me, nothing more.)

The paratroopers in the mountains had crumpled clothes and stubbly chins. One was eating a massive sandwich, the rest had pipes jammed in their teeth and big grins for the cameras. They made me think of Rich, who'd sent us a pic of him and Stumpy all in camo gear posing by a jeep. Had any of the German paratroopers in the web photos known Peter Schäfer?

We found pictures of the monastery being bombed the day after Valentine's Day, and hunted down black-and-white film footage of it, along with a German propaganda film showing soldiers looting – I mean 'salvaging' – treasures from the monastery before it was destroyed. We discovered there were four battles of Monte Cassino. The third battle started in March, when the Allies turned the town of Cassino into a lifeless wasteland. Busy month, March, what with Vesuvius blowing its top too.

'Check it out,' said Craig. 'The big Allied attack in February didn't work so on March fifteenth 1944 in only three hours more than one thousand tons of bombs dropped on the town of Cassino. It says that works out at five tons of explosives for every German in the town. Five tons! That's how much it took to kill each para! Bet it would take *ten* tons for Rich. Not that he'll get bombed.'

'Good to know,' I said, to hide the sudden lump of fear that choked my throat.

As usual Craig blathered on without stopping to think what exactly he was saying. 'When the aerial attack stopped, the artillery started. Blimey! It says here it was an inferno. What's that?'

'Look at the pictures.'

The town was all ground-down rocks, fire and smoke.

Craig whistled. 'No one could survive that.'

For once I had to agree with him. March fifteenth wasn't a good day to be in Cassino.

The Wrong Way

March 1944

A thin line of daylight trickled through the glassless windows of an abandoned house at the foot of the mountain. Peter flicked open his knife and quickly sharpened a point to his pencil. He had a precious sheet of paper and a few quiet moments to write home about his new promotion to Lance-Corporal, which meant three silver eagles on his collar.

March 15th. Dear Mother,

He paused. Had the others heard the noise? They were having bread, jam and schnapps for breakfast. Yes. They all tensed and looked up. Incoming Allied planes. Bombers.

'How many?' asked Sergeant Mahler, as if he were setting a school exam.

Heini's voice wasn't so steady. 'My God, *all* of them, I think!'

Wrong answer, thought Peter.

He stuffed pencil and paper away and scrambled for his kit.

'Do we go down to a rat run?' Erich asked. 'Dive for a cellar?'

'No time,' said Mahler. 'Follow me . . .'

They kept close to the sheer wall of rock at the base of the mountain. The first bombs fell. Erich whistled for Winston and the little dog came bounding after them. Mahler got to a cleft in the rock, the opening to a cave that engineers had blasted to make a bigger shelter.

'Further in! Move up! Muzzle that damned dog!'

Another cluster of bombs crashed into the town. Boom after boom echoed round the valley, like an almighty thunderstorm.

'There goes our breakfast,' said Erich, then he staggered as the mountain shuddered. Peter pulled him deeper into the cave. No more jokes or bravado. This was no ordinary raid, this was every ton of explosive in the world dropping on the town! This was an army of giants stomping them to pulp!

Hour after hour he crouched in the darkness, expecting every moment to feel the mountain tumbling down on top of him. No air. No light, just screaming missiles and pounding bombs. It wasn't only the cave walls that shook. Every bone in his body trembled. Snot ran out of his nose and he was in an agony of shame to be crying like a little boy, like a baby. The cave entrance collapsed. Several men passed out.

After everything else, it was too much. He couldn't stand the clamour, the fear any more! *I want to be home again. I want to be in my room, on the farm, at school even, anywhere but here . . . Make it stop! Make it stop! Make it stop!*

On one side of him Jupp was sick, twice. The smell was vile, worse than the stench of urine pooling the floor. On the other side was Erich. Always Erich. An arm linked through his arm. A hand took his hand. Squeezed it.

'Hold fast, Peter,' came a whisper in his ear. 'Hold fast.'

Eventually the deafening roar died away, followed by a silence so profound Peter wondered if there even was a world outside his own head. Words trickled into the void. A major was moving among the wreckage of the battalion, passing out schnapps and tobacco for anyone with hands steady enough to fill a pipe.

'It's midday now. They'll be moving infantry in under cover of the smoke. The b——ds will think we're all dead, but it takes more than a few bombs to finish off the *Fallschirmjäger*, right?'

'*A few bombs?*' muttered Lanky, slapping the sides of his head to get his ears working properly again. 'You'd think they'd run out at some point, but no.'

Eric coughed up dusty phlegm and spat on the floor. 'The Americans are so generous they'd strip off and throw their boots and braces at us if that ever happened.'

The chatter stopped as the major spoke again. 'Undoubtedly almost everyone who didn't make it to a shelter is dead now. We're here. Some will be in other caves and cellars. The enemy will expect us to be broken, defeated; dead or ready to surrender. That's not what's going to happen.'

'Can we defend this cave?' asked Mahler quietly. 'There are so few of us.'

'No, Sergeant, we will not defend this cave. We are going to spring a counter-attack!'

'Attack?' came the murmured response from every corner of the cave. The very word made Peter feel drunk.

'Attack! Outside will be a devastation of ruined buildings – a sniper's paradise. We'll find the best vantage points and liaise with any tank crews that have survived in the shelters we built. We have grenades, mortars, flame-throwers full of fuel. Most of all we have an utter determination to resist any attempt to win this town. The Allies must not take Monte Cassino! Remember our first commandment: *You are the chosen ones of the German army. You will seek out combat and train yourselves to endure any manner of test. To you, the battle shall be fulfilment.* So now we go, out of this cave and into legend. Move out, you devils. Move!'

Slowly, painfully, Peter joined the rest of the paras straightening up, shaking out their aching limbs and checking weapons. They stepped out of the cave into a broken world. No building unbroken. No stone pristine. No streets clear.

Like spirits they moved through the town, unseen, sacking tied to their boots so they went unheard too. 'Keep watching where Winston won't go,' Erich said. 'That dog's got a nose for unexploded shells and mines.'

Heavy rain began to fall, sludging up the rubble dust. The platoon scrambled up on to the first floor of an old bank. Erich went belly-flat on the floor with a machine gun pointing to where the street had been. Peter was right at his side, wedged against a broken wall and a filing cabinet full of scorched paper.

Let the enemy come, he thought. He'd be ready to fire – if he could just get his hands to stop shaking. Smoke curled through the ruins. Rubble shifted. Buildings crumbled. When would the Allies come? The waiting was worse than actual combat. He wanted to *do* something. To kill, if that meant he could live a bit longer. His mind wandered, back to idle hours in school when lessons had been boring and all he'd wanted to do was go off for a run, or go skiing, or meet Lisa at the cinema . . . He wasn't that boy any more. He was a paratrooper. The best. Invincible. *In this sign victorious.*

'It's just like the Spartans,' he said at one point, shifting to the other side of the filing cabinet to peer through a gap in the wall.

Erich looked confused. 'That Russian soccer team?'

'No, the Ancient Greek warriors, you know, at Thermopylae. Three hundred defenders against thousands of Persian invaders.'

'I wish we had three hundred. Even *one* hundred would be nice. How many of us d'you think are left in the ruins?'

'The principle's the same. We've beaten everyone back so far, massively against the odds. We'll do it again. The Spartans had a motto: *They shall not pass.*'

The other soldiers nodded. This was something they could relate to.

Erich repeated it. '*They shall not pass.* I like that, Prof. Like it a lot. I guess your schoolbooks are good for

183

something. In fact, if that pathetic sprinkling of bombs is the best the Allies can come up with, I've got to say I've had worse canings from my old headmaster, especially that time I—'

Peter never knew what schoolboy crime Erich was about to confess to. There was a hiss, a moment of horror, a metal scream tearing through the smoke . . .

A solitary mortar slammed down, hurling Peter backwards. He was rammed by the filing cabinet. It bore the brunt of the blast. Deaf, blind, too stunned to move, he lay trapped in a silent nightmare, mouth open, no words coming out. Blood poured from his ears. When his sight slowly returned he saw only a mist of red spots.

That was it. Erich gone. Last words.

He reeled, inside and out. Sensed familiar bodies around him. Arms pulling him. Schnapps trickling into his dry mouth. The floor had fallen. When he finally got upright he found he could step right out on to the street, so he did.

He left his gun, his kit, his reason behind. His legs were walking, his hands were tearing his helmet off. His head was bare to the cold torrent of cold rain. His mind was blank.

'Schäfer! Get back here!'

Voices echoed. More shells were whining in the sky.

'Come back! Come back! *You're going the wrong way!*'

So be it. That was the way he went, stumbling through the smoke and rain, straight towards the advancing enemy.

Missing in Action

Going the wrong way.

Halfway down the street I realised I'd passed our house. Walked back. Don't know how long I was standing outside at the front gate that day in March, before Dr Shepherd came out and found me.

I thought it was going to be all right. I really thought I could just go to school and carry on and things would somehow be all right.

Next thing I know the old lady had thrown a hairy blanket round my shoulders and she was pushing me into her kitchen where it was warm and cosy and smelled of fresh bread.

'Sit by the radiator,' she said. 'Ignore all my socks, they are drying.'

I couldn't. I had to look at something. Red socks, blue

socks, stripey socks, spotted socks . . .

She had an old-fashioned kettle with a whistle and a tea-stained pad for lifting it off the gas. She made me tea with lots of milk. I looked around the kitchen some more. Counted the bright bullets on the spice rack. One, two, three, four, five, six, seven, eight . . .

'Are you warm now?' she asked.

'I'm fine.'

'Why did you not go in the house? I have a spare key from your mother. No more glass-breaking!'

'I've got a key.'

'You are waiting for someone?'

'No.'

'Then you did not want to go inside because your mother is angry with you? No, she is not home yet. You are afraid of something, yes? Here – the handkerchief is clean. You can cry.'

'I'm not crying!' I took the hanky and blew my nose on it. 'Thanks.' I figured I had to tell her sooner or later. Dr Shepherd's one of those people who wear you down until they get what they want. In this case, The News. 'I didn't want to go in, in case there was a letter or an answerphone message.'

'Bad news?'

'*More* bad news, actually.'

187

She sort of hissed in a breath. 'Not your brother?'

One and the same. I blew my nose again. 'Mum got a call yesterday—'

'Wait!'

She went over to open the door and called out, 'Craig! Come through the hedge, your sister's here already.'

Poor Craig. His world was more bombed than mine. I wish I could've hugged him, he looked so sad, dragging his school bag along the ground. He got his own cup of tea. I sipped mine for the first time. It punched me in the mouth.

'What did you put in this?'

Dr Shepherd shrugged. 'A drop of whisky. Good for shock. *Allora*, tell me what's happened to Richard.'

'We don't know, that's the problem. They just said, *Missing in Action*. Mum went to the regiment base today, to speak with the family liaison officer, or someone.'

'Missing in Action.' She said the words as if trying them out after a long absence.

'It doesn't mean he's dead,' said Craig.

'Dead? Of course not!'

I said, 'Paratroopers do get killed though. Like Peter Schäfer.'

How quickly her face went white when she heard that, as if someone had turned on a tap to drain the life away.

'Peter? Killed? Absurd! Who told you that?'

'You did,' said Craig. 'You said the boy who wore the insignia died. We looked on the computer about all the battles at Monte Cassino and it was at the start of the third battle the town got whammed into the ground.'

'Oh, you mean . . . Yes. Cassino. Where the German paratroopers really became a legend, coming out of the ruins to fight back. *The Green Devils*, that's what they were called. Even the Allies admired them.'

I had been mad at Dr Shepherd going on about the old war when Craig was slumping deep down in his school uniform. Now I saw him perk up a bit and I realised she was deliberately distracting him. She might be mad but she was clever mad . . . and kind. When she put one of her thin hands on top of Craig's pudgy mitt I saw that too.

'Missing in Action only means a problem with communication,' she explained. 'The soldier exists somewhere, but the officers don't know where. Simple. Peter didn't die in that bombing raid. When he went missing no one knew what was going on – such chaos! If you ever feel even *one* bomb nearby you will understand. Cassino suffered thousands that day in March. There was no day or night, just yellow smoke. There were frogs, how do you say, *croaking* in the rain and little fireflies dancing. Bats, shadows, strange shapes – everything grey and yellow, including the ghosts.'

'Ghosts?' came Craig's shivery voice.

Oh not ghosts again, I thought.

She was serious. 'What else could they be? The town was in ruins but these people still came out of doorways, climbed stairs, and leaned out of windows when there weren't even walls. Children ran with rubble this high on their legs.'

She demonstrated with one hand against her knee.

'The children should all have been evacuated,' I said.

'They were.'

'But Peter saw them?'

'He saw something.'

'He must've been hallucinating. Don't people get shellshock? Or that post-traumatic stress thing?'

'Back then they said *bomb happy*, and yes, of course Peter was affected after so many of the bombs. That place, Cassino, it was one of the worst in the war. No one remembers now. They talk about D-Day and the fall of Hitler but—'

Craig interrupted, 'He did come back from being Missing, didn't he?'

'Peter? Yes.'

'Really?'

'Eventually.'

'What happened to him? Was he captured? Was he injured?'

'Yes and yes,' she answered, with a strange twist of a smile. 'The important thing is, Missing in Action only means *missing*. It certainly does not mean dead. Have hope. Where there's life there's hope. I am sure you will hear good news about your brother soon.'

Her gaze slid away and I realised she was slipping out of Normal into another struggle to organise her thoughts. It was scary to see how quickly she lost coherency.

Time is running out . . .

'Is your husband in?' I asked straightaway.

'Don't worry about him, dear,' she said. 'He's upstairs resting before tonight's performance.'

I tried again to catch her attention – anything to stop her going cuckoo. 'How's Winnie?'

'Winston?'

'No, Winnie. Your dog.'

'Here, girl!' called Craig. 'Can I take her out for a walk? We won't be long. I bet she'd love a scamper down by the river.'

Dr Shepherd smiled and nodded. 'I'll fetch the lead.'

Well done, Craig, I thought. You've headed off another bout of dementia or whatever.

Premature congratulations.

All she brought back was the crumpled parcel of paper and the jumble of objects, green *Fallschirmjäger* insignia included.

'Here you are,' she said, pressing something into Craig's hand. It definitely wasn't Winnie's lead. It was a pale piece of rock, full of air holes, really light to hold. 'It is pumice,' she said. 'Rock from the volcano. From out of the mouth of hell.'

Crossing the River Styx

March 1944

There was a river just like the one he'd read took people across to hell – the Styx. From the look of all the bodies in the water, people had just waded into it without waiting for a ferryman or even a boat. Should he follow?

He couldn't see the far shore, his eyes were dazzled. Brilliant stars burst in the yellow darkness. There were stars in the dark water too, stars and stripes. American flags. American bodies. The air tasted vile. Nearby explosions tore the sound of his breath away and blew metal grit into his skin. He cowered low, on his knees in marshy ground. If the shores of hell were so horrific what would hell itself be like?

Something butted his leg. He saw his hand was being

licked. He flexed his fingers and grasped something real, something warm and wiry.

'Winston! Are you dead too?'

The dog barked once and struggled free. Did that mean yes or no?

Peter staggered to his feet. Slipped into a crater. Came face to face with a drowned tank and the milky-white eyes of the tank crew, who were floating in a film of petrol. Winston yipped again and nipped at Peter's boots. *Not that way, this way.*

They both floundered further along the flooded riverside. Bullets were parting the fog to find them. The water was a shock of cold and the current was strong. He was too heavy. Stiff hands fumbled with buckles. He let his webbing fall. Winston floundered. Peter seized the dog's neck scruff and somehow swam on, keeping them both afloat. They sank into mud on the far bank. Were swallowed by it.

More man-made meteors came shrieking across the sky. Winston ran on ahead into shadows, so Peter ran too, one boot in front of the other, imagining he was Jesse Owens chasing a gold medal at the Olympics.

The wrong way!

Days and nights passed. Still he scrambled on, lips turning blue and face shrinking on to bone. There was always another hill to crest, more rocks to tumble down. He shrank away from any sign of other humans. Winston slept curled on his belly or went hunting for small creatures with crunchy bones. The dog lapped at puddles and barked at thunder while Peter shivered and bit the skin around his nails.

The clouds tore open for a moment and he saw stars, then a mountain exploded and fiery words were written in the sky. Back his mind went to the classroom again, to a slide show about Vesuvius. The Romans had no word for volcano. His cracked lips mouthed the Latin.

Mons igneus. Burning mountain.

He saw strange shapes in the smoke that bulged and billowed thousands of feet above the volcano crater – demons, eyes and eagles. Ash began to spread across the sky, drifting for many miles. Fire spat out and lightning flashed. A rain of grey began to fall. Grey fields, grey paths, grey sky. Grey soldier.

Somehow he got close enough to be looking up at the monstrous eruption. Waves of dense black cloud tumbled down the mountainside. Burning rocks fell like dying comets, making trees and bushes flare with flames then crackle and die. Myriad streaks of smoke trailed up from the ground – white snakes dancing on their tails. Falling cinders were like brandy-snaps burning holes in his uniform and making his skin sting. Larger rocks came arching out of the volcano as if tossed by contemptuous giants. When they landed they cracked stones or bones, whatever they hit first.

Not far now, he thought. He meant to walk all the way to the mouth of the underworld but it was already creeping forward to engulf him in the shape of a red-black flow of lava.

The edge of the inferno was very busy.

Why were there dirty little boys in hell, running up close to the red-black river, getting their hair sparked, then running away whooping? Why were there ambulances in hell, khaki-green ones parked at the end of long skid marks in the ash? Who were those men cresting the high ground with faces shielded from the intense heat? Why was there a village with grey geraniums still sprouting from window boxes?

Peter couldn't shake his head free of all the bombs going off inside. Suddenly he ducked down, sensing he was in someone's sights. Shrinking against a wall he looked up, expecting to see the jagged glare of Monte Cassino monastery. Wrong mountain. Volcano. Sniper? He reached for his gun. No gun. No one fired. A rain of rocks came down instead, hot, light missiles that crunched underfoot – pumice stones.

The nightmare became more crowded. He passed people loaded like mules, carts heaped with tables, beds, boxes and even a baby's battered highchair. Why were they trying to escape from hell when there was nowhere else to go?

The main street was a garish sight. At the far end a high wall of lava inched along, cracking stone with heat alone then smothering whatever it oozed over. A church dome had been severed from its proper mooring. It sailed slowly down the street on the dark tide. *Flash!* A camera bulb exploded.

Winston whimpered and shrank close to his legs.

Peter pushed through masses of people thronging near the lava's edge. Some, all in black, were on their knees praying. Some waved banners. Priests in ash-grey gowns sprinkled holy water as if to cool the lava's blistering heat. Two gaudy giants were dancing in the air. They were statues, one with arrows piercing his body, the other with pieces of pumice tearing his velvet cloak. *Flash!* Another camera shot. A woman with ash-and-blonde hair was taking photographs of the gaudy tumult.

'San Sebastiano Salvatore!' the crowd moaned. 'San Gennaro Salvatore!'

Peter staggered forward, waiting to feel the ancient fire lapping round his legs. Perhaps the heat would burn away memories. Just a few more steps and Hades could have him once and for all.

The way was blocked.

A soldier was there, looking straight at Peter as if nothing else existed. His face was as grey as ash. He looked old and heavy with sadness. He rested one hand on the pommel of his sword and beckoned with the other.

Can you help?

There were no footprints in the ash, nothing certain to follow. The soldier only showed clearly when the lava cracked open and glared red.

Come with me.

It was a command of a sort, the first he'd heard in days, so Peter gave himself up to side streets and uncertainty until he spotted the old soldier again outside a shabby café. There were no customers, only chairs burning at flaming tables. Paint on the café sign peeled in the heat. Peter flinched as overhead wires snapped, sending hanging streetlamps smashing into the café walls.

Come closer. Quickly. There.

One stick-thin arm was reaching through the wreckage of a house next to the café, just a few steps away from the angry lava flow.

You must help her, the old soldier said. *I cannot let any more die.*

The Burning Mountain

March 1944

A patch of green wallpaper, a square of yellow curtain, a sea of red-black lava.

A tabletop, a chair leg, a crumpled human body.

A girl, pinned down under a long beam of wood.

'Out of the way, Winston, I need to pull her free.'

Peter climbed on to the pile of rubble. Walking on ruins was second nature now. His boots barely skidded.

The little dog danced round and round in the street, now barking, now whining.

'All right, my friend. I'm doing the best I can.'

Dear God it was hot in hell! His body was melting in a river of sweat. His skin felt sizzling and his hair crackled. He saw he'd have to get the girl free, and quickly.

Already the beam end nearest the lava was blistering. For a moment he gazed, fascinated, as the livid, living rock crawled closer. If a mountain could bleed, this was what its blood would look like. Then he braced his legs and seized one end of the beam. His fingers burned. The girl gave a short scream as it shifted.

'Keep still!' he called.

'*Aiuto!*'

Every muscle straining, he tried to lift the beam again. It was impossible. The beam was too heavy, he was too weak. The mountain, it was everything – such a great angry mass, so hot, so powerful. How could one person defy it?

Courage, came a voice. The grey soldier was there again, with a spray of fire and pumice as his backdrop.

'I can't lift it.'

You have to lift it.

He took hold of the wood again and spat out every swear-word he'd ever learned. The beam moved, a few meagre inches to one side. It was enough. He dropped to his knees and began pulling the girl free. Eyes wide and body shaking she was like a panicked animal in his arms. He held her tightly, suddenly amazed that here was another human being, warm, real, solid enough to touch, alive.

Alive?

Together they tumbled down the building wreckage and on to the sloping stone street, where a solitary saucepan had been dropped and abandoned. Winston leaped on the girl in an eruption of fur and saliva.

'*Zecca! Zecca!*' laughed the girl, or was she crying? It was all Peter could do to hold on to her. She was small in his arms and so thin he could feel her ribs. He stared down at her. *I know you* . . .

'What . . . what are you doing here?' he stammered. 'Are you . . . ?'

Dead?

Was everyone he knew converging on hell? He looked around quickly, half expecting to see Mother trudging up the street, Father waving from a blank window, Sophie riding her bicycle to the lava's edge, singing nonsense rhymes in her high voice . . .

Vittoria unleashed a babble of Italian.

He shook his head, letting loose a cloud of ash flakes. 'I don't understand.'

'You ask what am I doing here?' she shouted, in German this time. 'God in heaven with all the angels and, what do you call them . . . ?' She mimed a circle round her head.

'Halos?'

'Yes, halos! What a question! How do I know what I am doing here? Enough that we have a war, then *il vulcano* wakes up! *Can you help?* asks Justinius, so here I am, helping. I pull stupid people out of their stupid houses. I rescue saucepans, sewing machines, *i piatti, i gatti, i bambini* . . . then that *maledetta* house fell on me . . .' Her words disintegrated into Italian again until she finally realised who she was speaking to. Her face mirrored his own surprise. 'What are *you* doing here, paratrooper?'

He had no answer to that. Pumice stones kept pattering down. The lava was getting closer. They should go, quickly. Go where? No idea. Away from danger. Was there any such place? The whole world boiled with catastrophe. How far could he walk? Was Vittoria hurt? She clutched her side as she coughed in the ash cloud.

'In here,' he said, pulling her to the shelter of a doorway plastered with lurid posters advertising some Italian film.

A new voice bellowed in competition with the volcano's roar – English, not Italian this time.

'Oi! You two! Get away from there! It isn't safe!'

He looked up to see a big man glowing red in the light of the lava, a man with sergeant's stripes and a medic's armband.

'All right, lad, I'm here to help. Is she injured? Let me look. She's conscious, that's good. Take her back to one of the ambulances and get her checked over. Are you even listening, mate? AM-BU-LANCE, you dozy swine.' The sergeant got close enough to see Vittoria properly. Recognition. 'Hey – I know you! You're the lass from the hospital, with the gold . . . I bloody know you too,' the sergeant spluttered next, staring at the silver eagles on Peter's collar. 'A mucking German paratrooper!'

A name formed in Peter's mind, something from a cloudless day in another life. Sergeant Joe Sharpe. Monte Cassino.

Flash!

An explosion of light. Peter raised his arm to shield his face. The photographer was there again, rolled-up hair, neat dress, red lipstick . . . the way women used to look before the war. The sergeant looked round just for a moment. Seconds enough for Peter to dart through the double doors behind him, following Vittoria.

He clattered straight into a row of wooden chairs, all set facing one wall, waiting for an audience. He scanned for another exit. Ran to the back of the hall. The air was stifling! There was a sound of stones and tiles grinding against each other. The stench of sulphur was vile. Little pieces of pumice skittered through a gap in the roof and streaks of dim red light shone on a small screen half covered by drab curtains.

He was trapped in a cinema.

Straightaway his mind went back to Saturday morning showings of *Flash Gordon*. Sitting with pals chewing strings of liquorice and fat boiled sweets bought by the bagful at the kiosk in the foyer. Cuddling with Lisa in the cosy privacy of a full-length feature film . . .

He heard the doors swing shut behind him. Then open. Then shut again.

Rasping sounds – Sergeant Sharpe clearing his throat of ash.

'I only want a chat. Just got a couple of questions for you and that girl. Where are you?'

In the half-dark Peter made his way to the back row, where Vittoria already crouched low behind some chairs. He put his finger to his lips. She put her finger up too. The middle one.

Then came a woman's voice, calling something in Italian. Peter caught the word *pericoloso*. He knew that one. *Dangerous*. The cinema shuddered. Greedy lava licked the baking walls.

The sergeant called, 'Come on out, Fritz. You'll fry if you stick around here.' He began to yank chairs aside to search row by row. 'I'm not letting you scoot off

Scot-free. We don't shoot deserters, you'll just end up in some cushy camp waiting for the war to end. Just come out!'

Unintelligible words. Peter felt for his gun, grenades . . . nothing there. The knife it was then.

This way, whispered a voice in his ear. Vittoria? No, she was already creeping towards a grey figure in the far corner of the hall.

Too tired, he thought abruptly. *Just want to stay here and rest*. His body felt like a bag of bones loosely gathered under brittle skin. His eyes closed. At least it was warm . . . almost snug . . . he could stay and watch a film . . . flickering figures in black and white . . . the story of a boy who left school to become a hero, rows of medals on his chest, everyone cheering, everyone smiling as he settled down to sleep oh so peacefully . . .

Something tickled his throat. Eyes open. Eyes down to see a grey sword point notched against his neck. Eyes up to see the old soldier who'd called him to help in the first place.

On your feet, soldier. Move!

An order, plain and simple. What could he do but obey?

Waiting

So what could we do but wait? That was the worst bit. We sat at home wondering when we'd hear any news. Was Rich alive? Was he . . . dead? I was aching for the phone to ring but when it did I covered my ears in case it was bad news, and then I'd listen and it'd be Aunty Pam, or the fridge repair man or some stupid drone selling double-glazing. Who cared about all that?

I found Craig with his face buried in a sofa cushion.

'Why are you crying?'

'I'm not!'

'Of course not. What's up?'

He said he felt lousy because he'd been texting Tariq and forgot all about Rich then suddenly remembered and hated himself for forgetting. I knew the feeling. I put Rich's photo on my phone wallpaper so I could look at it all the time. I had this crazy idea I'd forget what he looked like. I kept playing with the gold Roman coin, flipping it over and over my fingers till it was warm, playing *heads he's alive, tails he's alive*.

I read more about Roman Pompeii. Pretty depressing stuff. Not enough that you die in a horrific volcano eruption, but then little rocks called lapilli land all over you, and there's ash everywhere, so you get buried. The ash goes hard and sort of moulds over everything, even your clothes. Then, nearly a couple of thousand years later, you get discovered by archaeologists who pour plaster of Paris into the gap where your decomposed flesh was, to make a cast. Finally you're put on display in a glass case so tourists can get a gruesome kick out of your final moments of agony. If you're unlucky, the plaster starts falling off and your skeleton shows through. On some casts you can see tiny details in the plaster, right down to sandal straps and toenails.

A funny way of making life – and death – last for ever.

Intriguing though. If I was in a volcanic eruption they could get a plaster cast of me hunched in front of a computer screen, creased school uniform, messy hair, all of it.

Part of me wished we could just pack up and head for Italy, go see the sights, get away from it all. Dr Shepherd never mentioned Italy when we went round now. 'Eat this, drink that,' she said. 'Sit there, listen to music, watch TV, walk the dog, why not help me in the garden . . . ?'

'I'll fetch your groceries while I'm at the shop,' said her husband. We didn't let him. He was still a bit shaky after his time in hospital. I bumped into him on the way back from school one day. He was heaving a big black case off the bus. He dropped it on his foot but didn't yelp. I helped get it on to the pavement and waited while he caught his breath.

Gravity seems to drag old people down. Mr Shepherd was supposed to be tall but his shoulders were hunched over and his spine was bent a bit. He had nice blue eyes at least and he always looked smart, wearing a shirt and tie even when pottering about in the garden with his wife.

'I thought I'd save money on the taxi fare,' he confessed. 'Not very sensible. No, no, I can take it now. Could you pick up my newspaper please? Many thanks. Always bad news, isn't it? Back in the war they only printed good news. I wish they would trust us to know the whole story. Perhaps then we could make up our own minds what to think, wouldn't you say?'

'Is there anything about the war?' I asked.

'Which one! No, of course you mean Afghanistan. Your brother. No information yet? No? I'm so sorry. I wonder if war is hardest for families at home, the mothers and fathers and sisters waiting for news. You write to your brother, yes?'

'What's the point if he's missing?'

'Write to him anyway,' he said. 'Remember that wise Roman philosopher who said, *Where there's life there's hope.*'

'What if there isn't life? It's been days since Rich went missing.'

His mouth twisted. 'Sometimes even then there is hope, believe me. Well, here we are. Thank you for your company along the street. One moment, let me find something for you . . .' When he pulled his gloves off to search his pockets, I noticed how scarred his hands were. Not the hands of a university teacher, like Dr Shepherd.

He saw me looking.

'Burn tissue doesn't look so nice, does it? These hands have done a lot of hard work in their time, and you should have seen the bruises I got when kicked by the first cow I tried to milk!'

'You were on a farm?'

'As a child, first, then for many years I was worked on a farm not far from here. A good job. Good people. Big music fans. They let me work, which is what I wanted, and they played concerts on the radio every evening. What a sensational sound that was, when I heard jazz for the first time! Now, look, these are for you and a friend.

Perhaps the boy you mentioned before, yes? The one you wanted to go courting with.'

His hand was shaking as he reached into a coat pocket and passed me two slips of paper. Tickets for a gig. Some band called the Silver Eagles.

'You don't have to . . .'

He waved my objections away.

'Take them, take them, we are neighbours. Remember what I said about writing!'

Why not? Later I got a stack of blueys ready.

Dear Rich,

I expect you're back at base now, safe and sound. Hopefully. I looked at Afghanistan on the satellite map, it's very rocky. Funny to think you're there and I've never been anywhere. Is it still cold in the mountains? Have you had any more snow? It's rubbish here, just rain. I've been reading about the Roman city of Pompeii, not for school – that's one big YAWN – but it sounds strange, a whole city just covered in ash and pumice and left there. Pumice is really light. The lady next door showed us a piece she said was from Vesuvius in Italy but she could be making it up. It erupted in the middle of the war in 1944, not many people died and some villages were covered in lava. It went on for days and days, they said it was a spectacle. It

hasn't blown up since then. Are there volcanoes where you
are? Hope they don't erupt. We're looking after next door's
dog loads now. The fish are fine. We're fine.
Luv u
D x
PS. Write soon OR ELSE!!

Pretty short, I know, but they don't give you much room on the blueys unless you write really small. Anyway, what else was there to tell him? Just that we were scared he was never coming home, not unless it was in a coffin with a flag on it, like the ones they showed on TV, in black cars with soldiers marching after them.

You never really bother about people round you when they're alive and suddenly WHAM they might be dead and you find yourself thinking all sorts of crazy things, even sort of praying. Asking the great big empty space of the universe, 'Can you help?'

I made a kind of deal with whatever's up there. If Rich is still alive, I promised, I'll do anything. *Anything?* came this little voice in my mind. *Even do what the mad neighbour wants?* Even that, I replied in my mind.

And if Rich was dead? If he was dead I'd be gutted I never got the chance to see him one last time – to say goodbye. Maybe he'd come and haunt me.

211

City of the Dead

March 1944

Eyes in the tall trees. Eyes ahead, in the ruined tower and strange jags of stone. Eyes staring out from empty stone doorways where only shadows should have been. Vittoria saw no people as they stumbled out of the grey fields and on to an uneven street. No people, only eyes.

Behind them, Vesuvius still growled. What was German for volcano? *Berg brennand*? Burning mountain. All those lessons with a governess hadn't quite prepared her for the vocabulary of catastrophe, had they?

Peter skidded on the ash and pumice. When he fell he almost pulled her arm out of its socket.

In a mess of German and Italian she snarled, 'Get up, you stupid pig-faced Hitler boy! If you don't move

212

I'm going to leave you. In fact, I'm going anyway. *Du bist zu schwer!* Too heavy! What are you even doing here? You're miles behind the Allied lines. Don't you have dogs to steal? Jews to kill? Get up, *assassino*, killer, get up! *Raus!*'

She pulled him. Shook him. Kicked him. Kicked him again. Nothing worked, he just lay there. Like her his lungs rasped and his eyes were raw red from the ash that still drifted down from the cloud at the volcano crater. Should they shelter in one of the narrow little houses on the roadside? Anything had to be better than crawling along the exposed street. At least they weren't being followed . . . as far as she could tell.

She pressed one palm against her chest and tried to catch her breath. Her skin was torn and bloody, her whole body felt bruised and her ribs were so sore. Trapped in the collapsed house at San Sebastiano she thought she was as good as dead. She'd called and called for help but no one came . . . until this grim-looking soldier-boy came and hoisted her out. She looked round at the jumble of grey buildings, back at the sky-high mass of Vesuvius, then down at Peter.

'Walk some more, you stinky sack of bones, unless you want the British to find you and shoot you like the dirty deserter you are. Come on! We're nearly there.'

'Nearly where?' he whispered. 'What does that sign mean – *Via delle Tombe*?'

'Try to learn the language of the next country you invade. I don't know enough insults in German.'

'Oh, yes you do . . .' Another fit of coughing shook his body.

Useless weakling. Why did she have to be stuck with him? Just as well he didn't realise the sign meant Street of the Tombs, because he looked ready to give up the ghost and need a tomb of his own. While he rested she ripped a length of cotton from the bottom of her dress, tore it in two and passed one half over.

'Stop looking at my knees. Put that round your mouth, it might keep the ash out.'

What a horrible way to die, she thought. Breathing in ash till it set like concrete in your lungs. Was that how it had been for people when Vesuvius erupted in Roman times?

She heard a voice murmur in her ear: *Death comes as a fast-flowing wave of burning poison . . . Come this way and a little further.*

A few paces ahead the soldier Justinius blended with the ashfall. He was only a hallucination, she knew that. More fool her for listening to him when he said her help was needed on the mountain. His urgency – his

214

imaginary urgency – had been so convincing she'd hitched a lift from Naples and joined the army of volunteers helping evacuate people from the villages on the volcano's slopes.

And look where that had got her! Buried in a building, rescued by a half-dead German deserter and following a figment of her crazy brain into one of the very places history had most certainly shown *wasn't* safe from Vesuvius.

Pompeii.

Peter mumbled, 'They're looking at me . . .'

'No one's looking at you!'

'In those houses . . . Crowds of them in the houses, like a forest of hollow trees.'

Vittoria felt her heart quicken as she scanned the tumbling stone tombs. They were houses, that much was true. Houses of the dead, in the city of the dead.

Here, said Justinius. His words were like wisps of ash in the grey air. *This was once the pomerium, dividing living from dead. Broken by the volcano. You must cross it.* He gestured to the ash-grey land ahead, ridged with walls and streets. *The children screamed. Can you help? Can you help? Boiling sea. Roaring horror. Pain for a moment, then . . .'*

'*Ist es ein gespenst?*' Peter asked.

'A ghost? Don't be stupid!' she snapped. 'Only idiots and babies believe in ghosts. Look – it's just streets and ruins and streets and more ruins and . . .' She stopped. Eyes were now looking out of faces. People were clustering ever closer to the line of the pomerium, as grey as the sky, as grey as the ground, the walls, the empty spaces. Old, young, men, women, children, babies . . . there were too many faces to focus on.

She began to pull back. 'I don't think we should . . .'

Too late.

Peter was up on his feet again, and waving at a streak of half-dark nothing flickering in the gateway to Pompeii. 'I know him,' he murmured. 'That lad there, by the archway. He was on the convoy when we retreated to Naples. Hey, you!'

'Hush!'

'He was on the truck, I never knew his name. And that American, we didn't think he was going to make it. The medic must have fixed his neck. He was so heavy on the stretcher. And there's the boy from the monastery, next to the old granny, his eyes aren't bleeding any more. And all those men in uniform . . . can't you see them? Hey, you there . . . wait . . .'

'No, *you* wait.' Vittoria laid a hand on his arm. 'Who are you talking to?'

216

He shook her off. 'I have to go after them.'

Yes, said Justinius. *Follow me, I'll take care of you now.*

Vittoria hesitated. Were there really people flitting through the streets? The only one she could see for sure was Peter, and even he was beginning to look hazy. German idiot, showing off how brave he was, trying to make her look like a coward. She wasn't afraid of any ruined city!

Back straight, chin up, she crossed the line of the pomerium and walked under the tallest of the three stone arches into the town itself.

At first she kept her eyes low, looking for Peter's footprints in the ash. The main streets of Pompeii were made up of large blocks of stone, uneven now and worn to grooves where wheels must once have rolled. There were raised pavements but she didn't trust her footing close to the high kerbs, not when every surface was blended to a fragile, drifting layer of grey. There were also broad stepping-stones blocking the way. She discovered the first of these when she walked into it.

New streets led away from every silent crossroads. She'd no idea Pompeii was such a complete city, for all that the walls were now half-high and well-worn steps led up to nothingness. Not as big as Naples, but a fair-sized town all the same. How many people had lived

217

here once? How many had died here? House after house, street after street, she seemed to be drawn deeper into the maze of ruins. Broken columns stabbed the air. Trees grew, great dark things marching in a line. She stopped in one doorway and saw speckles of ash blow aside to reveal mosaic words on the floor: CAVE CANEM.

Beware of the dog, whispered a voice.

And a dog barked – surely a dog barked, or did she imagine it? When she ran along the street to follow the sound there was a dog, a scruffy, wiry mongrel dog, stiff with bravado before a new doorway.

'*Nit*, you silly mutt. There you are! I thought we lost you coming down Vesuvius. Did you stop and bite that pig of a sergeant? Thank God in heaven you're all right.'

Nit growled. Not at her, but at a shimmer of grey within the house. With one hand clutching Nit's furry neck Vittoria peered inside . . . and leaped back. There was another dog, bristling on the end of a chain, barking soundlessly. Beyond the dog was a girl in a short tunic. And a boy. And a man. And a woman. And more people wavering in the shadows, all drifting like torn silk . . .

She backed into the street.

The street was full – a crowd of people simply looking at her. Nit gave a little howl then sat down to scratch behind one ear. The crowd swayed and parted. There, up ahead, wasn't that . . . ? The familiar bent back, the wrinkled hands, the rheumy eyes . . .

'Nonna! Nonna! I told you to stay in bed – I *told* you! I was only going to be gone for a day or so, to help the people on Vesuvius. Nina was meant to look after you. Nonna, come back! Wait! I don't want to be here on my own. Which way should I go? All the streets look the same. Nonna, wait, I can't keep up!'

More grey faces clustered round.

'Go away! What do you want? I can't help you.'

She saw through them to a patch of grey grass growing round tall brick shapes. Bread ovens. A bakery. Was Nina here too? And Mama, perhaps, and Papa? Come from Rome to take her home?

Then she saw it. A dull red devil face grinning and bobbing up and down. Strings danced. The puppet waggled.

'Diavolo! Oh thank you Jesus!' She reached out to embrace the boy but he danced back, jerking the puppet with him. 'It's all right, it's me – Vittoria. Queen Vittoria, remember? I'll look after you now, everything's fine. I can't believe you're here! I thought you were . . .'

Dead.

The truth stabbed deep.

Diavolo. Dead from typhus fever over winter. Buried in

a grave without a headstone, without a name.

She squeezed her eyes closed. Let her *not* see Mama or Papa! Let Nina *not* be here. Let there be no one else she knew. Let there be no ash, no ruins, no rumbling volcano. Let her wake up safe in her bed at *Casa Sanfelice*, with little Nit curled up at her feet.

Her eyes opened on the same grey cityscape. Before her a vast structure now loomed, edged with monumental staircases and pierced by a dark tunnel. Stumbling into this blackness was a boy in German uniform.

Should she follow him? Of course not. She did anyway.

The tunnel was strangely warm. No ash fell. She still had the sensation of her fingers brushing something soft. Not Nit's fur, though Nit was trotting along at her heels, the pelt of larger predators moving past. It brought to mind stories from her governess, tales of Roman times when beasts were let loose in an arena, when men fought to the death and sand soaked up the blood. This, then, was the amphitheatre at Pompeii.

She kept her eyes on the circle of grey at the end of the tunnel. The air flared out into a wide, flat oval ringed by tier upon tier of stone seats. Each seat seemed to hold a spectator. All looked towards the centre of the arena where Peter stood, turning round and round as if utterly lost.

'Vittoria! Did you see him? He was right here. My friend – Erich. Do you remember him from Naples? I thought he was . . . I mean, I don't know. Do you know where he's gone? Lance-Corporal Erich Bergen. The first leave we get, he's going to take me round Berlin. I saw him – right in front of me all the way here, only now . . . Erich!'

The name fell flat on the ground, no echoes. No reply.

Didn't he realise? Deluded idiot. For all his uniform and silver eagles he was no better than one of the war-orphan waifs wandering the side streets of Naples.

Someone called her name. *Ave, Vittoria Venafro!*

Gaius Justinius Aquila. The old soldier was limping up a set of stone steps to the centre of a bank of seats. A grey audience had flowed through the arcades of the amphitheatre to fill the seats. Now they all rose to face him. He held out a grey arm and pointed at Peter, who looked like a ghost himself, half in the land of shadows, waiting to be claimed completely.

Come, the crowd whispered. *Come and join us. We are many. You will not be alone.*

Peter swayed. His legs folded and his body fell to the floor. He was still. The crowd shivered.

Nit gave a sad bark and skittered over to the boy, nuzzling the ash-clogged hair and limp body.

'Leave him, Nit,' she began, thinking, *he's dying*, then telling herself it didn't matter, it would just be one soldier less. One ghost more. Clearly there was nothing she could do. How could she help? She didn't care anyway.

So why was she kneeling at Peter's side all of a sudden? Cradling his head in her lap? Wishing she could blow life back into him – anything not to be left alone in such a hideous place . . .

His eyes opened. They still looked blue, even in the grey light. His face felt horribly cold to touch. His words cracked as he forced them out. She bent lower.

'What? What are you saying?'

'Latin. From gladiators before a fight. *Ego moriturus te saluto.* I who am about to die salute you.'

'Die? Don't be stupid. You're not going to die. I won't let you.'

Everyone dies . . . The words rustled around the crowd.

Vittoria covered her ears but couldn't keep the whisper out.

. . . dies dies dies . . .

Yes, since the war there was death on every corner. Bombs, fever, starvation, it all ended one way. Not without a fight, though! Night after night she'd sat up with Diavolo during the typhus epidemic that winter,

222

laying cool cloths on his hot body, shielding his eyes from even the dimmest light. The boy himself had been desperate to hold on to life, right up to the very last shuddering breath. She was every bit as defiant. If this was a dream – a nightmare – or hallucination, then she would bend it to her will!

Peter stirred and got to his knees, still in a daze but now reaching out for Vittoria, for Nit, for anything that felt real. He mumbled again.

'Enough Latin,' she snapped. 'Talk sense!'

He almost smiled at her. 'Try to learn the language of the next country you invade.'

'Tell me what it means.'

'It means, where there's life . . . where there's life . . .'

'. . . there's hope, yes? Where there's life there's hope!' Quickly she turned to shout up to Justinius. 'You brought him to help me, didn't you? When I was trapped? I would have been smothered in lava – burned, killed – if he hadn't pulled me out. You don't want to keep him, he's nothing special. I should know, I read his diary. He's just a boy. Can't you help?'

Help? Justinius shimmered for a moment.

'He doesn't have to die yet. Help!'

Life is not given to us for ever, Vittoria.

For ever for ever for ever, echoed the crowd.

'He can have it for a bit longer, can't he?'

By way of answer, Justinius raised one arm straight out with the hand in a fist, the thumb pointing to the side. Despite his lumpen face and simple tunic he looked like an emperor. Slowly he twisted his fist. A decision. The thumb turned . . . *down.*

Where would the death blow come from? Would it be a thrust to the guts from the sword Justinius always carried? Or would it come creeping stealthily, or surge like a sea of ghosts to smother him . . . smother them both?

'What are you waiting for?' she shouted.

There was a ghost of a smile from the old soldier above them.

The thumb goes down to show weapons must be dropped. The signal is not for death. His life is given back, a loan only. What is taken must one day be returned.

The Bath House

March 1944

It was the same dream every time. The crackle of fire, the screams of demons falling out of the sky. He was holding a mountain on his shoulders, it turned to lava, the whole world burned. Erich was lying next to him, smiling and happy. Peter tried to call out a warning but he had a mouth full of ash. He was made of ash, nothing but ash. Vittoria was there, tearing pages from his diary, wafting the paper so the breeze began blowing him into a thousand grey flakes . . .

He couldn't hold the mountain up any longer. It fell and crushed him.

He still had eyes, so he opened them. Still had a nose, it was bleeding. Still had fingers, splayed them. Touched rough rocks and wool blankets. Saw rose petals waving over his nose. A nightingale nestled in the leaves of an orange tree. There were jasmine bushes, laurel wreaths and fat plums hanging in bunches. Olives looked ripe and ready to eat, ivy twined round everything. He reached out to pick a fruit . . . and found it was only painted on to the wall, just like the fountains, trellises and elegant temples.

'Pretty, isn't it?' came a voice.

Blankets shifted and rocks jostled as he moved. He saw Vittoria Venafro, sitting as straight and tall as if on a throne. 'You're here.'

'*Certo*. Obviously.'

'And Winston . . .' Peter gave the dog at his side a gentle stroke.

'Winston? Oh, you mean *Zecca*?'

'What's *zecca*?'

Vittoria shrugged. 'My German lessons did not include names for all the insects that live on dog skin, and look around, there is no Italian-German dictionary here. Before you ask, this is a house in Pompeii. It is midnight on the twenty-fourth of March. The mountain is still burning but I think the worst could be over. You have slept for two days.'

'Am I alive?'

'Just.'

There was a moment when he caught a glimpse of other dreams. Of grey ghosts in an arena and a thumb turning downwards. He shook these memories away.

'I feel awful.'

'You look it.'

'What's that noise?'

Vittoria paused to listen. 'There is no noise. Pompeii is closed to tourists at night.'

Peter rubbed his head. That's what was wrong. It was quiet. He hadn't heard silence since . . . for ever. No bombs. Nothing.

Vittoria wanted to know why he'd called the dog Winston.

He said, 'Because of Winston Churchill, the British Prime Minister.'

'But Zecca is a female. A girl.'

Winston was a girl?

Winston gave a happy yip.

Peter took the metal canteen she offered and drank deeply. The water was better than any fine wine.

'The Roman water system is still working,' she said. 'There are . . . what do you call them in German . . . ?' She mimed a pumping action.

'Pumps?'

'Those. On the corner of the streets. I found the bottle and food in a house near the city walls, with some other things.'

'You stole them?'

'Other people shared with me. They just didn't know it.'

He didn't care. He was so hungry he could have eaten his own arm. He wolfed down great mouthfuls of bread, beans and tomatoes.

'*Stupidotto!* You'll be sick!'

She was right. He retched up sludge.

'What . . . what is this place?' he said eventually, focusing on the fact that the floor was high and very uneven, made up of hundreds of pieces of pumice. Only the top part of the garden painting was visible on the walls. The ceiling looked more like the underneath of the world, complete with roots poking through. It was stained black from lamp soot, and he spotted half a dozen fat terracotta lamps burning. They looked like real Roman lamps. Perhaps they were.

She said, 'Justinius . . . Someone . . . showed me how to get down here. Archaeologists haven't discovered it yet.'

'What now? Will you call the police?'

She said something about the police in Italian, then turned to German again. 'You can stay here or do what you like. I'm going back to Naples. I've got twelve children to look after these days.'

'Twelve? All yours?'

'Mine? I'm fifteen years old, you potato head! You smell *molto forte*. You must have a bath before I go.'

He looked around for water pipes and taps. 'Where?'

'The bath house, of course!'

They had to crawl to exit the buried house. Outside the evening sky was still trickling with ash. He wrapped his arms around himself to stop the shameful trembling that began as soon as he was out amongst the grey ruins. She'd think he was mad, fearing to see ghosts in every shadow. She'd already think he was weak and useless because he had to hold on to the walls as he walked.

'We have a bath house back home in Bad Kohlgrub,' he said with pride. 'Like the Romans.'

She wrinkled her nose. He shut up. Why should he apologise for his filthy state? Everyone knew Germans were civilised, for all the Romans had called them barbarians. And she was no picture – torn dress, hair like a bird's nest, dirty bandages round grazes on her legs. Not such a fine lady now!

The bath complex covered a whole block of the town. Vittoria led him through ruined rooms, past stone shelves for clothing, past a broken pool for bathing, into a silent chamber studded with patterns on the floor and walls. Ash slipped through broken ceiling arches. One lamp made a circle of smoky light. He tried to imagine a thousand lamps lit, slaves padding over the mosaic floors, the scent of perfume, sweat and oil all involved. It was quiet now, much as his ears strained for the sounds of sport in the exercise ground, the grunt of Roman masseurs.

She hadn't been joking about having a bath. The stubborn mare had actually lugged in a battered tin bath, stolen from God knows where, then filled it, presumably from the water pump. Nearby, rocks were baking in a small fire she must have started earlier.

'Take off your jacket,' she ordered. 'Is that the right word – jacket? I need something to hold these rocks.'

How clumsy he felt, struggling with buttons. He pulled his paratrooper jump smock over his head and passed it over. She wadded it up and transferred the hot rocks to the bath water. It steamed enticingly.

Hurry up in there! his sister Sophie used to shout on Sunday evenings at home, when he lay in the cooling water reading books or just staring at the ceiling dreaming of flying.

'That's a good trick with the rocks,' he said.

'It's important to be clean.'

'Why are you being . . . friendly?'

In an instant she turned on him and rattled out an angry mix of Italian and German.

'I am not your friend. My father was a Jew. You killed him in Auschwitz. I am half a Jew. Your enemy.'

Auschwitz? What was she talking about now? He'd never heard of the place, let alone killed anyone there. She was raving. Foreign. A thief. This all started with a robbery.

'You stole my diary. Where is it?'

'I burned it.'

Burned it? 'That book had my letters, my photographs!'

'*Lasciami!* Get off me! *Dio!* You are so dirty you need a flame-thrower on your skin, not soap. Put this powder on after the bath, to kill . . . insects. I'm going outside. Now wash!'

He flushed a little. His uniform was stiff with mud and heaving with lice. He'd worn it continuously for so many weeks, getting undressed was like peeling a skin off. For a while he just stared at the bath, then he dipped a finger in to watch the ripples. His blistered feet nearly died to be warm again. Ash, mud, blood, worse, it all swirled into the water . . . Sinking into the warmth was

231

all he needed of heaven. Every bit of his skin sighed. There was hardly an inch of his body that wasn't bruised, scarred or just plain battered.

He held his breath and submerged completely . . . and woke from a dreamless doze to hear Vittoria talking. The water was dirty enough for modesty at least.

'You look better clean, Peter Schäfer. You have one hair growing on your chest. What's that picture?'

She was pointing to his shoulder, to a black eagle tattoo. *In this sign victorious.*

'All the men in our platoon had one done back in Berlin, before we flew out.'

'You should've stayed there.'

He didn't answer. He was thinking, *Where is my platoon now? Erich'll be wondering if I'm all right.*

She tossed him a shabby shirt and trousers. 'These were left in a storeroom. Americans accidentally bombed Pompeii last September, so things are a mess. Your Nazi uniform should be boiled. Or burned.'

'I'm not a Nazi and I'm not ashamed to wear my uniform. Give it to me.'

He got out of the bath and used some fresh cold water from the can to rinse off, keeping his back to the girl of course. It was good to be in clean clothes, but only until he'd found and killed every louse on his uniform.

He turned round again. 'What about you?'

She scowled. 'What do you mean?'

'Don't you want to wash? I'll heat fresh water.'

Every movement was painful, from tipping the dirty suds away, to filling more cans with clean water. He was nervous going out of the bath house to the pump in the street, expecting an ambush, snipers . . . God knows what. But the air was still and nothing came to kill him. No moon showed through the ash cloud. Vesuvius was as dark as the night and therefore invisible, save for scratches of red in the sky above the summit. He went back into the bath house and played hot potato with more rocks from the fire.

Vittoria's hair was an ashen thicket, very different from the sleek black gloss he remembered. She'd acquired a comb and a pair of scissors and was obviously trying to decide which would work best. He watched her try the comb. It snagged – she was lucky to find it again. She took up the scissors, held out a hank and prepared to cut.

'Wait!' he said.

'What? You want the scissors? Please, cut your throat with them.'

'You're too kind. Why don't you wash your hair first, then see if you can salvage anything?'

She frowned. Did she understand him? Eventually she knelt at the side of the bath, obviously meaning to dip her hair in and scrub, there was just enough soap left for that.

He hesitated. It would be a good time to slip away, taking whatever he could carry. The moment passed. He rolled his clean sleeves up, took a mug, filled it with warm water from the bath and poured it over her head. Filled the mug again; poured it again. Then he took the soap to gently wash and rinse her hair.

For some reason, she let him.

Night Hunt

March 1944

One morning, a few uncounted days later, when Peter woke there was a small parcel on the blanket and a cold space where Vittoria had been sleeping, wrapped in a stolen overcoat and curled in his arms.

He opened the parcel warily. It was his diary, not burned after all, only somewhat vandalised. He touched every letter and ate every photograph with his eyes. Mother, Father, Sophie, Lisa . . . Erich.

How strange, to read the things he'd jotted during training and on the dreary flight from Berlin to Rome. *Let the storm break loose!* he'd written on one page. What a thing to wish for. It had. Furiously.

He stretched out and smiled. No longer in an

underground room, he and Vittoria had found a rich Roman house to eat in the evening before. They'd walked through the dark rooms and cool colonnades, holding stolen candles to light the faint paintings that still clung to the ancient walls. At the centre of the house was a garden with a solitary tree. Next to the garden was a dining room – three stone couches around a crate he'd pilfered from a storeroom near the Roman forum. Food, also stolen, had been set on the crate – bread, cheese and wine.

As they ate he'd told her of the great Roman feasts he'd read about – swans, flamingos, giant turbot, fried dormice and caraway cakes smothered in honey. She didn't understand most of the words. She'd imagined more modern food – real ice cream, and dishes of steaming pasta loaded with pieces of fat fish and sprinkled with curls of Parmesan. He would have been in heaven having a loaf of his mother's home-made rye bread served with pickles, and potatoes fried in pork fat, with a side dish of hot cabbage and onions . . .

Good God, was he hungry already? Was there anything left to eat?

It was getting chilly – twilight again – so he pulled the blanket round his shoulders and warmed his hands over an old oil lamp that was still softly burning. He flicked through his diary once more. The pages opened at a page of poetry by Martial – *Live for today. Too late is tomorrow's life.*

A good motto to tell Erich when he got back.

What about Vittoria? Where was she now? Thieving? She was elusive, one minute warm and letting him hold on to her, next minute all imperious and touch-me-not. Last night she'd been almost agreeable, tossing him a packet of stolen cigarettes with a careless, 'Happy Birthday'.

'How did you know?' he'd asked. She'd looked smug. Now he guessed she'd seen the date circled in his diary – the thirtieth of March.

So that had been his birthday feast. A world of difference from the cake and candles the year before. Would they be missing him, back home? Better they thought he was . . . dead . . . than the truth – that he'd deserted in the middle of a fight. Some hero. Perhaps he should be dead, but he felt far from it – fantastically alive, in fact! Alive and bursting with . . . with long-suppressed energy. He'd had to keep himself still, the last few days, not wanting Vittoria to notice how his heart raced when she was close.

He tucked the diary into his tunic. Time for another cigarette. He hoped she'd be back soon. It would be so nice to stretch out and talk some more. To tangle his fingers in her long, dark hair . . . to reach forward and perhaps kiss the lips that so often curled in scorn. No! She wouldn't open her arms for a German. A coward. *Assassino*, she'd called him. He could guess what that meant.

He lit one cigarette with the lamp flame and carried the rest out to the street. He breathed the smoke deep into his lungs but it tasted wrong – reminded him of other places and people. *So here I am*, he thought. *Sixteen years old, standing in a ruined town with no right to be alive, and yet, I am, very alive! Wanting to stay that way. Wanting to stay here . . .*

He inhaled again. Choked. Reached for a weapon. Found he had none.

Dropping the cigarette he turned and ran from the big man advancing up the street.

'Hey! You! Stop!'

He didn't need to speak English to know what the man wanted. It was that damned medic from Vesuvius, Sergeant Sharpe from Monte Cassino with his spinning gold coin. The swine had somehow hunted him down – how was that possible? Not without help. Only one person knew he was hiding in Pompeii.

He darted off the street. Vaulted the low walls

separating a row of Roman shops. Dodged the dark shapes of ancient bakery ovens and crouched in a corner to catch his breath.

Which way now?

He edged towards a crossroads just as twin beams of light flared out from the town's forum, a wide grassy space fringed with columns and broken temples. An engine rumbled. Sharpe wasn't alone. There could be any number of soldiers hunting for him, thinking he was a spy. Police too, perhaps. Could they drive a jeep along Roman streets, or would it founder on the stepping-stones?

He ran on, eyes wide, ears keening for sounds of someone approaching.

Over here, came a voice. He froze. It was a grey soldier . . . the same one who'd helped him from the burning cinema on Vesuvius. Now the man gestured towards a low wall and a gateway. *Follow me.*

Peter shook his head.

'Come on out, paratrooper! Time to give yourself up.' Sergeant Sharpe's voice bellowed in the twilight. The night was warm. Ash still obscured both moon and stars.

This way, soldier.

This way, that way, following the man's limping

239

silhouette Peter was quickly lost in the city's dark maze. Soon he smelled trees. A line of grey figures, some old, some young, beckoned him towards a corner of a garden roofed over with corrugated metal. Training and instinct taught him how to take cover. Hard to say how long he hid, sandwiched between the plaster cast bodies of two eternally gasping children. His fingers itched to feel the warm barrel of a machine gun or the comforting bulk of stick grenades stuffed in his belt. All he had was his knife . . .

Electric torchlight flashed in the streets. A whole group of men were searching. Was that a woman's voice? *Flash!* His mind went back to the mouth of hell, to the photographer on Vesuvius. The same woman?

He tried to will his heart to slow down as footsteps scuffed ash along the street by the garden. More voices. What were they saying? Forget Latin, he wished he knew English.

'Look,' said the woman. 'This must be the Garden of Fugitives. Pompeiians took refuge here when the volcano erupted that time.'

'Watch the ruddy flash, you nearly blinded me,' said Sergeant Sharpe. 'Christ, those bodies look alive. They're just plaster casts, right? Dead Romans.'

Peter kept utterly utterly still. The torchlight swept

past him. Then the woman spoke again. 'Joe, is one of the bodies wearing a wristwatch?'

Click. The sound of a revolver safety-catch being released.

Instant reaction.

Peter leaped up and crushed a chunk of pumice into Sharpe's eyes. Tore the gun away. Held it, hands steady as concrete, muzzle pressed to the man's skull.

'Joe!' The woman was too stunned to move.

'Get back to the jeep, Maggie! You don't want a picture of this in your mucking magazine! I told you not to come.'

Who to shoot? The woman, to stop her blabbing? The man, for daring to hunt him down? Or should he try and talk, explain what he was doing so far behind enemy lines?

He thought of the paratrooper's third commandment: *Beware of talking. Men act while women chatter. Chatter may bring you to the grave.* Teeth clenched, he jerked his head at the photographer. 'Get out of here!' She understood enough German to stumble back to the dark street.

Sharpe made his voice sound calm. 'Put the bleeding gun down. It's the girl I wanted a word with. You can come and cool your heels in the clink till we find out what you're doing going AWOL in Allied territory.'

Peter couldn't understand why he wasn't pulling the trigger, why the man's brains weren't already spattered in the ash. *I am a paratrooper!* he thought desperately. *I should be shooting!*

Sharpe didn't wait to be shot. With a roar he stamped on one boot and seized the arm holding the gun so forcefully Peter was twisted down to the ground. The pistol fired.

Nothing happened. No bullet cracked through Peter's skull.

'No mucking bullets!' Sharpe cried, shooting eight times from an empty chamber. 'It was full! I loaded it myself! Come with me, you bloody hooligan.'

Peter fought hard as he was hauled along the garden by his tunic, burying the blade of his knife in Sharpe's leg, making the man bellow. Then a foul-smelling light suddenly flew into his face. A star? Sharpe let go of Peter as another light flared, then another and another, in a travesty of constellations. Soon there were about a dozen of these manic stars flitting about in jerky patterns, trailing smoke. Peter felt a surge of panic. He almost screamed when something brushed against his leg. Teeth nipped his calf, just above his boot tops.

Winston.

Good boy, he thought. *Sorry – good girl.*

The little dog only yipped and scampered off. Peter followed. Winston led him through the city and safely past any other searching soldiers. Peter tried hard not to wonder why Winston seemed to have a shadow, a grey dog that ran alongside her, passing through bricks and stones as if they weren't even there.

The city walls loomed high. Here the dogs sat and waited. Only one came close enough to be patted. A faint sea breeze blew ash from the sky and showed a dim spatter of genuine stars above the silhouette of the volcano. It reminded him of another mountain, burning many miles to the north, another sky and man-made stars that rained down explosions. Somewhere out there the lads of his platoon were hunkered down ready for the next onslaught. How could he have walked away from all of them? From Erich?

'Hands up!' came a familiar voice, soft in his ear.

Slowly he raised his hands as he felt something pressing into his back. 'Just shoot me then,' he said. 'I know you want to.'

'Shoot?' Vittoria laughed. 'With this piece of . . . what do you say in German? Rock?'

He turned round and she threw it to him. He caught it, looking around for British soldiers. Ready to run again. 'This is pumice. What's going on?'

She spoke with pride. 'My *scugnizzi* – the children – came. I sent a note to say I was safe in Pompeii and they came to help! The British are all distracted, lost in the city. If they find the forum their jeep will not be there. It has melted like ice under a hot sun.'

'Melted?'

'The parts are now stolen. We can sell them for a lot of money. Did you hear the children laughing? They made the burning *pipistrelli*, the bats. Is "bats" the right word?'

'Bats?'

'You put old cloth in petrol. Tie the cloth round a bat. Add fire. The bats fly away like stars. It is cruel, to amuse only children of lower classes, but a . . . distraction.'

'And now you get a reward if you hand me over to the authorities so they can shoot me as a spy?'

She shrugged. He didn't know whether to shake her or kiss her. He kept one hand on Winston and the other on his knife. 'Who was the woman?'

'Margaret? A photographer of the war. Nice but stupid. She only takes pictures, she doesn't think about people properly, or why would she be with that *porco goloso*?'

'*Porco goloso*?'

'Greedy pig. See, you are learning Italian fast. The sergeant was looking for me as well as you. He thinks I have gold.'

'He knows your reputation.'

'I was given the money! Then I spent it this winter, on food and medicine.'

He asked, 'Was it old money? Sharpe had a Roman coin from Vespasian's reign, I saw it.'

'Not any more. It is liberated now, here. Look! These too . . .' She reached into her dress pocket and pulled out eight shining bullets. 'He didn't know I was behind him in the dark.'

Peter stared. That explained why he wasn't now a bleeding corpse. To lift a gun, extract the bullets and replace it, all unnoticed – the girl truly was a queen of thieves. 'So you . . . you didn't betray me?'

Her chin rose, the arrogant little aristocrat!

'Someone else must have sent a report to the Allies, or heard there were fugitives in Pompeii. Not me. Justinius said, *Leave no one behind.*'

'Justinius? You mean, the soldier?'

'You . . . you see him too?'

How could he see someone who wasn't there? They both glanced round. Shadows . . . ash . . . something moving just on the edge of vision. Did he imagine a man's shape sitting on a fallen wall with one hand on the pommel of his sword?

Leave no one behind.

'I have to go back to Monte Cassino,' Peter said, at almost the same moment the thought came into his head.

Vittoria exploded.

'*Pazzo!* Lunatic! Don't you understand? The Allies are going to keep on fighting until they win this war. Everyone hates Hitler. Hates Germany. If every last Allied soldier dies fighting to get to Berlin then the women and children will make an army. You will lose the war – *you will lose!*'

He closed his eyes briefly. 'I know.'

What a thing to admit! To confess he no longer believed.

Vittoria looked as if she'd been punched. 'You are on the wrong side of this war but you go back and fight and die?'

'My friends are there.'

'Then you'll all die together.'

'Perhaps.'

'Go then – leave me! I don't care! *Vai vai al'inferno!*'

'Vittoria, I . . .'

He held out his hand and for a moment their fingers touched. Then she pulled back. What did he expect? A

246

passionate clinch? A kiss? A promise to write – to meet again when the war was over? Impossible.

There was a clink as she slipped the eight bullets back into her pocket, then she was gone, Winston too, leaving him with nothing but a piece of pumice. He looked for Justinius.

'You understand, don't you?'

Victor, vanquished, all die in the end. What endures is the legacy of how you lived. Come. I will lead you back to the burning mountain. I will help.

The old soldier rose and began to limp down the grassy bank towards the street of the tombs and the old Roman boundary between living and dead.

Peter followed.

Leave No Man Behind

I was upstairs in the bathroom when what do I hear but this savage chopping noise and what do I see from the window but my kid brother standing in a mound of hedge twigs, wielding a pair of rusty shears.

'No, don't look at me, watch what you're doing!' I yelled.

'It's a short cut!' he yelled back.

Fair enough. The last few months we'd been nipping next door quite a lot, especially since Rich went missing. Mum had aged a million years and threatened to quit her job to look after us full time – to which Dr Shepherd replied, 'Stupidity! We are here. I will cook. You find what has happened to your boy.'

'Gonna have to do more running,' Craig vowed after every slap-up meal over at number sixty-four. Pasta,

248

lasagne, pizza, steak, home-made ice cream. . .Heaven! Oh, and tons of salad stuff and veg too, which the old lady made us eat on pain of death-by-glaring. They thought they were looking after us, but they were both so doddery at times, I think we looked after them more.

Which was, strangely, just as nice.

They refused to sink into old age without a fight. *Live while you're alive*, was their motto. Dr Shepherd said that's why they kept the skull – to remind them how close death was.

I said, 'That's really gloomy.'

'No no no! Death makes life precious,' she cried. 'Pain can be a sign of love. You have pain for Richard more now you think he is in danger, yes?'

In a word, yes.

She tapped my heart with a bony finger. 'Where there is life, there is hope. Be sad if necessary, not before, *capisce*? Understand?'

Rich said pretty much the same thing the day he left home to go to war. He ruffled my hair (because he knows I hate that) and tossed out a casual, 'Don't worry about me, squirt. I'm gonna be fine. You just go on having a good time.'

A good time?! In the bottomless pit of dullness that was My Life until recently?

Rich was full of it all before he left, I remember. Bragging. Swaggering. Swearing (when Mum wasn't around). I was thinking, how come they give you a big gun to shoot when you can't even shave without cutting your face open? The camo-gear and weapons and everything make soldiers seem so big, but they're just skin and blood and bones underneath – big messed-up vulnerable tough guys. Maybe it took five tons to kill every paratrooper that time Cassino was bombed, but one bullet could kill a man too, even if it had taken a whole nineteen years to make him, like Rich.

Surely he couldn't be dead when he was so good at being alive? Rich was always careering round with his mates, having fun, playing tricks on me and Craig. Always bopping to music or running off to gigs. Never satisfied with nothing-much. Unlike me.

Was he dead already and we just didn't know it? Dead, or all mashed up in hospital? Had the army forgotten about him?

'They don't just, like, *abandon* each other,' Craig informed me.

'Listen to you, all knowledgeable,' I snapped back.

'It's true! *Leave no man behind*, that's what they say. Except in a race, and then it's tough if Tariq can't keep up.'

Craig and Tariq got entered into some cross-country championship. I thought it'd be better than mooching round the house, so I went along to watch – me, Mum, Dr and Mr Shepherd were there. The old bloke took Craig aside just before the race began and said something quietly, I couldn't hear what. Craig nodded, as if he'd just had tips from an Olympic coach.

I said, 'Try not to get trampled into the ground. As brothers go you're not that bad and I don't have anything black to wear to a funeral.'

'Ha ha, very funny, *not*.'

'It'd be funny if you had a sense of humour.'

'I do! I laughed when you walked into the patio door last summer.'

'That wasn't funny.'

'It was to everyone watching.'

'What'll be funny is watching *you* get beaten by all the rest of the runners today. Look at them – hulking big brutes, aren't they? Like androids specially created for the sole purpose of thrashing you at cross-country.'

That wiped the grin off his face.

There was a wicked sharp wind whichever way we stood. We shouted and cheered when we saw Craig amongst the pack of boys. Embarrassment probably spurred him on a bit, either that or we were seeing a miracle. Fact is, my little brother actually finished THIRD, I'm not kidding. I hauled him away from the rest of the mud-spattered lads.

'You weren't last! What did he tell you before the race?'

'Mr Shepherd? He told me to keep my head up and my arms tucked in for a more even running style . . . He said to imagine I was Jesse Owens going for gold at the Olympics.'

'Who?'

'Don't you know *anything?* Jesse Owens got four golds in the 1936 Berlin Olympics.'

Well there you go. No telling how often someone can surprise you with odd bits of knowledge.

As for me, I was determined to try a challenge of my own. Anything had to be better than sitting around moping and waiting for Bad News from Afghanistan. It wouldn't seem much to anyone else, but here's how I rated it on a scale of one to a thousand (one being a cinch, a thousand being excruciatingly close to impossible).

1   Breathing.

10   Getting a rise out of Craig.

100   Climbing Everest.

500   Finding a cure for cancer. World Peace.

1000 Getting a date with Gavin Parker.

'Already I told you, just ask the boy,' said Dr Shepherd. 'How is this difficult?'

'It's really scary!' I objected.

'Not as scary as a volcano erupting.'

'Well, no-o-o, but . . . what if he laughs at me?'

'Then you know he is an idiot.'

He didn't look an idiot, hanging out by the school gym with a bunch of mates, including Samantha I'm-a-Cow Green. Nipping off and admitting defeat was the sane option. Walking up and saying, 'Hi Gavin,' was PURE INSANITY. Hey ho – why not be nuts every once in a while? Here's what happened next.

Gavin looked surprised. 'Hey, Denise. What's up?'

'I've got tickets.'

'Yeah? What for?'

'This jazz band.'

'Jazz?'

'They're called the Silver Eagles.'

This was the point where he sniggered and turned his back on me . . . except he didn't. He shrugged. Said that sounded cool – where and when?

I HAD A DATE!!!

Guilt whacked me in the stomach harder than the look in Sam Green's beady eyes – what about Rich? Fear told Guilt to shift over and make room for Life.

I met Gavin at the pub where the gig was. He gave me a sort of peck on the cheek when I arrived. We were about to order Cokes, only who goes and pops up at the bar but Dr bloody Shepherd. Excruciation!

'You will prefer a beer or wine?' she said. 'Oh, no objections! On the continent the children drink a little. Much better than England where everyone drinks too much.'

'What are you doing here?' I muttered.

'For the music, of course!'

I wondered if it would be better to die before things got worse. I prayed, *Please don't let her sit with us*, and she didn't, thank God. (I thought, does that mean there *is* a God? And if there is, would he make Rich be all right?) Dr Shepherd went right to the front of the pub where all the band's clobber was set up on a stage. The drum kit had *Silver Eagles* written over it, and a slogan underneath the eagle picture – *In This Sign Victorious*.

Gavin said, 'These guys were pretty big in the Fifties and sixties. My dad's well into them. He had a jealous fit when I said the girl I'm going out with has tickets for their gig. This place'll be packed out tonight.'

Going out with . . . Now there's a phrase I could get to like.

The first aging rocker got an awesome round of

applause when he made it to the mike. Another geriatric shuffled on stage to tune up a trumpet. A beefy bloke took up a saxophone, and then my jaw practically unhinged to recognise the old guy on the giant violin type thing that Gav called a bass fiddle. It was Mr bloody Shepherd!

The penny dropped. No, treasure chests full of pennies dropped . . . cascaded down! That was the black box I'd seen him lugging around – a bass case!

Mr Shepherd came to the front of the stage and raised his hand in a kind of salute.

'*Ave*. Greetings! If you haven't heard us before, stick around, we're not so bad. We've been practising for many decades, I can tell you!'

Cue: laughs.

'Of course, we've played a lot of different venues in our time. Ever heard of the Cavern in Liverpool? We used to headline there, supported by four lads calling themselves The Beatles. I heard they did all right for themselves. Never gave us any trouble, but then we're not easily intimidated . . . an ex-para, an ex-marine, a former Polish bomber pilot and Greg here was the toughest of us all – a school bus driver.'

I grinned. Couldn't help myself. Gav was grinning too, so straightaway we had something in common. Then the band played. It was fantastic! I'm not into jazz or old music much, only this was brilliant, every note. We were on a total high right to the end and way beyond. Gav nipped to the gents so Dr Shepherd slipped over to say hello. She was beaming.

'They are *meraviglioso*, yes? Marvellous?'

'Yes!'

'So sad it is their last time playing, after all the years.'

'No way. The last time? Why?'

The tone of her voice dropped ominously. 'All we have is borrowed time, Denise Cooper. What is taken must be returned. Tick tick tick, the days disappear . . .'

I thought I'd better dash to the loo before she went off on another speech. When I got back to my seat Gavin was there first. He said, 'Your gran's really cool. She was just telling me all about your trip to Italy. I'm dead jealous. When are you off? And your grandad, he rocks!'

'Grandad? Oh, we're not related,' I said. 'They're just . . .'

Just what? Neighbours? Friends? *Who exactly were they?*

The rest of the evening was between me and Gavin. Let's just say I didn't think about Italy much when he walked me home. He said, 'So what amazing thing are you going to plan for me next? The Silver Eagles gig will take some beating.'

I went all airy. 'Actually it's your turn now, mate.'

He grinned. Possibilities!!

Then, wake up the next morning, Saturday, expecting it to be no different from any other day and there's NEWS! The phone call we've all been waiting for . . .

RICHARD IS ALIVE!!! Alive alive alive alive alive alive alive alive!

Much bouncing on sofa, running round and round the house and whooping!

Well, that's what Craig did. I watched Mum put one hand over her face and start to cry. She looked all grey and washed out. I don't remember what it was like when she heard our dad wasn't coming back from the Gulf.

Anyway, don't think about that. Think about Rich being ALIVE!

I texted Gav to let him know and he biked round to give me a big hug – most welcome.

Basically, the family-liaison-thingy bloke called to say Rich was picked up on the edge of a really rough area, injured – no details how – but cared for by a bunch of Afghani peasants . . . even though it was Afghan guerrillas who'd attacked him in the first place.

Dr Shepherd was *very* pleased when we told her about Rich but she didn't look surprised that he'd been looked after by the enemy.

'Sometimes civilians see past a uniform to a human

being. Peasants in the Italian mountains helped many soldiers during 1944 – Allied or German, wounded or deserting. They said it was simple hospitality. Did you know Peter Schäfer had help when he was lost in the mountains? Of course, he was a lunatic, going back to Cassino in the first place. I suppose he didn't know it would be in plenty of time for the fourth and final battle for Monastery Hill. On the way an old goat farmer gave him milk and bread, even though he was the enemy.'

'Yes!' barked Mr Shepherd. 'Then his own side tried to shoot him when he finally returned to the battlefield!'

'What do you expect?' said Dr Shepherd, giving her husband a poke. 'When they realised who he was they thought he must be a ghost . . .'

The Last Battle

April–May 1944

From one dead land to another.

No fields or orchards blossomed in the valley around Cassino, only green mould on lifeless faces. The town was even more ruined than Peter remembered. Wrought iron balconies jutted out from bedrooms that only ghosts could sleep in. Hooks for hanging baskets now held empty air. Blank windows, blank doors, flooded gardens. How could anyone be alive in such a shattered world? Instead of ash from the spent volcano, now he breathed in corpse gas and rock dust.

He drifted through the rubble of this chaotic graveyard catching glimpses of enemy soldiers snatching sleep in bivouacs, or simply nestling in stone shelters. He wondered which ones he would have to kill once he was back in the fray again. Which ones might kill him.

So many Allied men and machines were massing for the next assault!

'They'll outnumber us two to one,' he whispered to Justinius.

At least, was the grim reply.

'The German defence will hold.'

Perhaps.

'You think we should give up? Surrender? Do you want the Allies to win?'

Justinius wavered as a wind blew through the valley.

You are a soldier. You fight. The winner is the one who fights best.

'Am I a coward for running away before?'

The children cried. The sea boiled. I turned away.

Peter looked up at the mountain. The blasted monastery looked right back. Under cover of darkness he scrambled up the jagged mountain slope, crazy with fear that he'd stumble into an Allied position before he found whatever scattered paratroop platoons had survived. Stronger than fear was the urge to be with friends again – to see Erich and hear him laugh.

And there Erich was, silhouetted against the stars, helmet off and hair ruffled up.

Over here.

Peter climbed closer then froze, suddenly certain he was in the sights of a sniper rifle. Where could he hide? He looked around. No sign of Erich or Justinius.

A hoarse voice exclaimed, 'Who's there? Halt or I shoot!'

He knew that voice! 'Heini?'

Heini Holz didn't lower his gun, but he didn't fire.

'It's me. Schäfer . . . Turnip. Don't shoot!'

'Turnip? My God – back from the dead!' On Heini's signal other figures emerged from the darkness.

Who were these dark-eyed wraiths in ragged uniforms with skin the colour of mud and bone? They pulled him into their rocky shelter and swarmed round him for a vigorous welcome, lips cracking into wide smiles. Lanky Lutz Dullman, Max Klein, Jupp Weiss, the others, it was so good to see them all again, even Mahler – now a captain – who tried to sound stern despite the fact that several of his teeth and some of his cheek was missing.

'The prodigal son returns. Where've you been? Why didn't you send word you were still alive?'

Peter felt less like a paratrooper and more like a schoolboy hauled up before the headmaster for truancy.

'The bombing . . .' he said vaguely.

They all nodded. There was a crawling silence no one knew how to fill.

He cleared his throat. 'Where's Erich?'

Captain Mahler coughed. 'Bergen?'

'I saw him . . . Just now. He showed me where you were . . .'

'Don't you remember? Two weeks ago. The bombing of Cassino. You were there . . . the mortar . . . a direct hit.'

Heini frowned. 'You know Erich's . . . ?'

'Yes, yes. I know,' Peter said quickly, but his face was burning and his eyes were hot with idiotic tears. He knew. Of course he knew. He must have known all along. He could still hear the hiss of the shell hurtling down. Still see a mist of red spots hanging in the air. Erich was dead. *Stupid* of him not to remember, doubly stupid to show how much he cared now.

No one laughed at his sudden tears. No one called him a coward, or worse, deserter.

'Here.' Mahler handed over the green and silver paratrooper insignia saved from Erich's pack. 'He was a good soldier.'

Peter choked on an unexpected laugh and thought of a line from the Roman poet Martial: *To the ashes of the dead, glory comes too late*.

Lanky wanted to know where Winston was. 'Because I lost my St Christopher medal, rats ran off with the Captain's lucky rabbit foot and we're shafted without a mascot! I'm telling you, Schäfer, the Allies are killing themselves to obliterate this place and us. One damned mountain! There's only a fraction of our regiment left, you know that? Now the snow's melted there's no water except half a pint a day for washing and drinking.'

'We get oranges,' said Heini. 'If the mules even make it this far.'

'And mosquitoes,' someone else said gloomily. 'Spreading fever now it's thawing for spring. The civvies are keeling over and dying of Bad Air, they call it. *Mal Aria*.'

'Good to have you back,' they all said at some point or other. There were two new faces on the platoon, dirty faces, young faces – new recruits. Peter ignored them. They weren't Erich.

Hours, days, weeks. Attacks, counter-attacks, exhaustion.

Spring meant nothing to him. The sun was warm but he never saw it – daylight was too dangerous. Grass tried to sprout between the rocks. They trampled it underfoot as they moved from one jumble of rocks to another. No trees blossomed on the mountain, all were topless charred skeletons. No flowers survived the angry spurt of flame-throwers.

Flies buzzed, mosquitoes bit, soldiers fought.

Was every country in the world throwing soldiers at Monte Cassino? During one unnerving stretch of silence Peter found himself admiring the multitude of different rotting uniforms dressing the corpses piled around his platoon's position. Indians, Gurkhas, Moroccans, Algerians, French, Canadians, Americans, British, New Zealanders . . . the paratroopers fought and killed them all.

In the aftershock of every fire-fight he saw other shapes milling around the corpses. Grey faces with blank eyes that never blinked. Grey men in caps, helmets, turbans, bandages, whatever they'd worn at the moment life was torn away. It seemed as if an army of ghosts spread over every jag and crevice of mountainside, into every ruined building of Cassino, across every field and riverbank of the valley. He saw them most clearly by the light of machine-gun muzzle-flare or in the gritty aftermath of an explosion. He saw Erich quite often, always just too far away to touch. In the darkest hours he saw even more armies, dressed in uniforms of every century, all the soldiers who'd ever marched through the valley, whether defending Rome or attacking it.

Mahler caught him one time, staring past the mangled corpses into this multitude.

'Steady, Schäfer. Don't let your nerves go again.'

Peter didn't speak. How had his whole life, his whole world, been reduced to pouring so much blood into such a small patch of ground? He knew he'd carry on fighting, that wasn't in doubt. A man comes screaming at you with a gun or bayonet, you don't mess around, you fire your gun, you throw your grenade, you kill until it's safe to draw breath. He'd fight all right. He was just so . . .

Mahler laid a hand on his shoulder. 'There isn't a man on this battlefield who isn't afraid,' he said quietly. 'Anyone who says otherwise is lying.'

'Is it true the Allies are massing for another infantry attack tonight?'

'Polish regiments this time. Poland's not done well out of this war. They're taking this attack very personally. They hate Germany. Expect fanatics. Consider it a compliment – we've worn all the other Allied armies out. We will win, you know. We're the best of the best! We have to keep possession of the mountain, whatever comes at us. Remember: Ultimate Victory!'

The new night brought wave after wave of Polish soldiers crashing into German positions on Monastery Hill, a torrent of reckless heroism. They were met by a sea of fire from German flame-throwers and devils dressed as paratroopers. Peter's hair crackled in the heat.

His fingers burned as he fired the machine gun till all bullets were spent. Then he hurled grenades, one after the other. When these were gone, he threw rocks. Still the Poles came on.

'There's no ammo left!' he signed to Captain Mahler. 'We can't hold them off.'

Mahler froze like a teacher wondering whether to discipline an unruly class or retreat to the sanctum of the staffroom.

'What shall we do?' Peter shouted, more urgently. 'What are your orders?'

A single line of blood trickled along the ridge of Mahler's nose, then he toppled forward, dead from an unseen bullet.

Heini fixed his bayonet. 'This is it, then,' he muttered. 'I'll take a few more with me when I go.'

Peter's eyes were so swollen from grit and exhaustion he could barely see straight. When he did finally look around, he thought saw Erich beckoning him further up the ridge. *This way.*

He pulled Heini back from the advancing soldiers. 'I'm not dying till I have to! Drag whoever can't walk back up there, to that cleft in the ridge. Leave no one behind.'

There were other German survivors. They huddled together, strapping up wounds and doling out whatever

266

arms and ammunition were left. A few canteens still held water, this was shared too. Peter took a sip. Just those few drops were enough to remind him of soap and hot water in a Roman bath house . . . of a girl pouring wine for his sixteenth birthday. The night sky became blindingly bright as more shells blew the mountain apart. Despite the lull in the combat, he felt hope shrink into a small, dark place deep inside.

He looked around at his comrades. Less than a year before they'd gathered in an aircraft hangar ready to be deployed, with immaculate uniforms and unshaken faith in the Führer and Fatherland. Less than a year before they sang, one voice out of many . . .

Our numbers are small, our blood is wild,
We fear neither the enemy nor death.
We know just one thing: with Germany in distress,
To fight, to win, to die the death,
To your rifles, to your rifles!
Comrade, there is no going back.

No going back. The Poles now had the advantage of defence. The paratroopers were outnumbered, outflanked and exhausted. Low on supplies, low on ammo, low on anything but the will to win. Peter smiled in the dark and thought, *the greater the difficulty, the greater the glory*.

'Comrades to the death,' he whispered suddenly.

'Comrades!' they all swore in the darkness.

To the death, echoed the grey soldiers watching.

Nights and days lost meaning. Three times Peter joined the surge of assault on that crucial spur of rock. Lanky Lutz Dullman was shot during the first attack.

'I wouldn't mind so much,' he said, just before death took him, 'only I heard the Poles brought a bear with them and I really wanted to see it.'

More fell in the second attack. Max Klein was lacerated by shrapnel from a grenade explosion. He died without a word. Jupp Weiss's last words weren't fit to be repeated. Peter saw two new recruits die within seconds of each other. One stood on a mine seeded by his own side. The other, going to help, got a spray of bullets for his trouble.

Heini threw away a jammed rifle and swore. 'No officers, no captains, no sergeants even. What the hell do we do now?'

Newly promoted as full corporal, Peter remembered the eighth paratrooper commandment: *You must grasp the full purpose of every enterprise, so that if your leader is killed you can fulfil it.*

'We attack anyway, that's what we do.'

The spur was won back on that third assault. Too tired to celebrate, Peter helped pile up a new barricade of dead and dying and crouched low while more artillery smashed down.

Had there ever been a time when the sky wasn't ripped by the screams of bombs and soldiers? Had they ever eaten tasty food? Drunk clean water? Slept in beds? Was there ever a time when the air didn't reek of cordite and corpses? Now it was only possible to exist one minute at a time. Anything more than that – anything like living – was luxury.

Oh if you could only see me now, Professor Meyer, he thought. *Promoted to corporal. Awarded the Iron Cross, Second Class. Holding down a raving lieutenant from another regiment so the sole surviving medic can amputate a mangled limb using only my notched pocket knife.*

The operation was successful . . . for a day. The lieutenant died anyway, crying, 'Remember to tell Marie.' Peter watched the lieutenant's ghost stagger away into the smoke. Tell Marie what?

The paratroopers waited for the Poles to regroup and attack again. There was a moment, a rare quiet moment, when the ugly yellow pall over the mountain cleared in a welcome wind. Peter looked up. Through the gap in the smoke he saw a solitary bird – a beautiful golden eagle soaring free. His lucky mascot. His sign. In this sign victorious.

What was that line of Latin he'd had to write out a hundred times once, as punishment for talking during class? *Liberae sunt nostrae cogitationes. Our thoughts are free . . . Our thoughts are free . . . Our thoughts are free . . . Our thoughts are free . . .*

If only he could be free of it all too! Without meaning to he raised his head and straightened his shoulders for the first time in weeks. Suddenly he couldn't bear to be cramped and crouching any longer. He was desperate to stand at least, to walk tall, to sprint like Jesse Owens on the Olympic track.

He made it as far as standing before hearing a familiar sinister hiss. A nasty smell of burnt munitions scraped his nostrils. The mortar exploded.

No time to appreciate this was exactly what happened to Erich. No time to speak grand Last Words. Only time for one final thought:

I   don't   understand

Shrapnel

The day Dr Shepherd finally told us Peter Schäfer had been blown up by a mortar in the last battle of Monte Cassino, Craig was seriously outraged.

'You said where there's life there's hope!' he spluttered. 'You said paratroopers were tough. Leave no man behind. You *said*!'

'Hold your hosses,' I said slowly. Maybe I'm not, like, a military historian but that doesn't mean I can't think things through eventually. 'You just told us Peter's last words.'

'Yes, yes,' Dr Shepherd agreed. '*I don't understand*, he thought.'

'*Said* or *thought*?'

'Thought.'

'Well that's impossible. How can you know the last

thoughts of a dead man? Either you're lying or Peter didn't die.'

Her eyes! They flashed alive so brightly. I felt as if I'd won a million quid or something, she was so impressed.

Craig looked from me to her. 'He didn't die?'

By way of answer she went to her favourite packet of newspaper and passed him a nasty jag of metal.

'This is *shrapnel* – the same word in English and German. It was from the mortar that exploded on Monte Cassino. Doctors pulled it from Peter's head. Don't worry, they washed it. Lucky he had a thick skull.'

'That's . . . that's not Peter's skull under the tea towel is it?' (I'm glad Craig asked that, cos I wanted to.)

'Skull of Peter? Of course not! They gave it to me at Cambridge University when I retired. It is only a Roman skull from a burial in England. Nothing to do with Peter or Vittoria, believe me.'

'So tell us what happened next.'

'No!' she said. 'No no no.'

No? She's spun the story out over *months* and drops hints and clues and makes us work for every new instalment, then she says *no*?

Her face took on a sly look. 'I will only tell you what happened if you agree to help me.'

Craig asked, 'Help you look after Winnie? No problemo!'

Oh, she didn't mean dog-walking or house-sitting, I knew that. She meant a mad trip to Italy. She knew I knew. She was smiling deviously as she got up and went to her sitting room. She tossed a photograph on to the kitchen table, where we'd just been eating amazing pepperoni pasta. The photo landed next to the piece of shrapnel. It showed two black-and-white boys in uniform grinning for the camera.

'Peter and Erich,' she said needlessly.

Real people. She'd been talking about *real people*. I'd known it all along, only it hadn't actually sunk in. This war she was on about, the battles in Italy, the diseases and disasters and everything, it had *really happened*. Just like in Afghanistan, or in hundreds of other countries around the world, wars *really were happening*. How could that be true when we were just sitting in a house, in a cul-de-sac, in a normal town where nothing happened except rain and school and television?

Craig wanted to know if he could borrow the shrapnel to show Tariq. I wanted to know if I could borrow the photograph.

'Yes,' she said. 'Take it if you please. But make your decision soon. I tell you again and again, there isn't much time.'

Time enough to do a little digging, I thought. Time to prove I'm not a waste of space.

I zipped back to our house and legged it upstairs – straight into the bloody clothes airer, so I ended up plastered with Craig's running kit and Mum's tights. Being practically perfect, I took the time to set the clothes drying again, then slammed my bedroom door on the world and headed for my desk.

The inventory:

✓ One suddenly outstanding brain? *Check*
✓ One genius hunch? *Check*
✓ One German/English dictionary with slightly duffed-up corners? *Absolutely Check.*

Sounds from the landing as Craig followed me upstairs and collided with the laundry too . . .

'What are you doing?' he yelled.

'Bog off! Can't you read the sign on the door? The one that says PRIVATE – NO ENTRY TO BROTHERS.'

'The one that fell off and Mum recycled it?'

Oh God. Couldn't he tell I was on to something and just leave me alone for a mo?

I had a quick check of my phone messages because Gavin had been trying to call to fix up a trip to the cinema

– fantastic – then I propped up the old photograph of Peter and Erich, opened the dictionary at 'S'. . .and ran my finger down the columns till I got to *Schäfer*. I whooped. Kissed the photo. Even yanked the door open and kissed Craig. He yelped and fled. Silly boy. I was just about to tell him who exactly we were living next door to.

The Crypt

May 1944

Agony. Semi-consciousness. Delusions.

Killers. Pain. But no painkillers.

No morphine, no alcohol even, barely any water. Medicine was too precious to waste on men most likely to die, Peter knew that from experience. No bandages left either. He felt paper being plastered on to the shrapnel lacerations on his torso and limbs . . . pages torn from his own diary. His leather belt became a tourniquet strapped round his left thigh.

'Your leg!' someone exclaimed. He couldn't understand the fuss. His leg was fine – he couldn't feel it hurting at all.

They heaved him on to a stretcher and humped him

276

up the mountain to the rubble of the monastery. A headless statue was stark against explosive flashes in the night sky. Where the monastery basilica had once been there was now a hole going down to where a crypt was converted into a first-aid station.

He couldn't comprehend what he saw in the crypt. The low ceiling was arched in several places. Every inch of every curve was covered in amazing mosaics patterned with a rainbow of jewel colours. Peacocks spread their tail feathers, foxes ran between vines, saints sat in dignity and blessed unfolding lotus flowers. The word PAX was written in large red letters all around, just like the sign over the monastery entrance. Wide-span bird mosaics had him struggling to whisper, 'Eagles!'

In this sign . . . He blacked out.

They set him down. Left him to wait his turn, take his chance. Corpses were stacked against every wall. Eventually a medic and an orderly squeezed through the bodies to look him over. The orderly raised an eyebrow. The medic shook his head.

'Not much chance, but it's a clean cut through the shin. Couldn't've amputated it better myself. He's young. Too damn young. Still, where there's life there's hope.'

Peter heard their words even though blood gummed his eyes.

'Cicero,' he murmured. 'Cicero said that.'

They sealed the stump of his leg with something hot and vile so he passed out.

Minutes, hours, days, he counted none of them. He heard flies and felt the ghost of his left foot. Flinched as plaster dust showered down during particularly heavy bombardments. It reminded him of ash falling and he dreamed of a girl with black hair and mocking eyes. There were rattles and gasps as men died. Soon only a handful clung to life, Peter included. *Not ready yet*, he told the grey man who sometimes hovered between candlelight and darkness. *You'll have to wait for me*, he told Erich, when Erich also came to visit.

One day he woke to hear music, a heartbreaking horn melody played in the ruins above. It stopped abruptly and there was silence. Proper silence – no guns, no mortars, no grenades. Unsteady footsteps crunched on the stairs down to the crypt and there was the sound of someone starting to cough and retch. A second man followed. They both skidded in pools of filth as they crossed the crypt floor. Peter squinted in the gloom. He made out uniforms with Polish insignia.

The monastery had been taken. The enemy were here. He had no weapons, no strength even to defend himself. Would they shoot the few survivors one by one or simply leave and toss a grenade into the crypt?

One of the Polish soldiers went back to the stairs and stood in the weak light. He shouted a single word.

'*Medic!*'

Peter struggled to keep conscious as help came. His stretcher was lifted into daylight. Sunshine! Warmth, light . . . the absence of explosions. His friends were gone. All the Germans who could walk were gone. The retreat must have happened sometime in the night. He was set down gently on the mountainside, feeling like a very feeble remnant of a once mighty army. The sky truly looked like heaven. Only one thing marred the brilliant blue – the red and white of the Polish flag flying over the monastery ruins.

In the distance he could see a stream of men and machines. Brits, Yanks, Kiwis, Aussies, Indians, Poles . . . mile after mile of Allied troops passed through the conquered valley on their way to Rome. The monastery watched them go. The war moved on. Monte Cassino was yesterday's news.

The Polish men were drunk with victory. One, a captain, came to crouch at Peter's side. Peter held himself still, expecting spit, insults or a cold knife blade. Instead he found his hand being gripped in sympathy as a medic came to ease away the wadding over his many shrapnel wounds. The captain was an old man – in his forties – with sagging skin and eyes that had seen everything. He spoke German well. He said, 'I had a son your age.' The haggard look on his face told the rest of the story.

'What will happen to me?' Peter asked with cracked lips.

'Hold fast,' the enemy captain said.

Hold fast, whispered grey ghosts before they disappeared, burned away like mist in the morning sun.

PAX

May 1944

Vittoria was utterly disgusted with the Allied POW hospital on the outskirts of Naples.

'All this for prisoners of war? A comfortable bed. Antibiotics against blood poisoning. Quinine for malaria. Lice lotion. Luxury! Now, are you sure we have the right ward?'

Margaret Bentley-Wyke made a very convincing nurse with a clean apron, a clipboard and a smart leather Gladstone bag. Her Italian was improving.

'According to the list I saw, this is the place.'

'Well then, what are you waiting for?'

'Are you sure . . . ?'

Was she sure? No. Absolutely, no! Not sure but . . .

strangely excited. And a little concerned that her starched linen headdress was on back to front. No time to check that now, not when her accomplice was getting cold feet. She put on her best victim-of-war look and whispered, 'Remember the children!'

Ah yes, the children. Twelve photogenic orphans who'd star in Margaret's next article about the Italian campaign. This was the journalist's incentive for helping now . . . that and the deluge of guilt Vittoria poured on her regarding the small matter of aiding and abetting Sergeant Joe Sharpe's hunt for gold in the ruins of Pompeii.

'I had no idea it was about looting Roman treasure,' Margaret objected. 'When he said there was a German spy in the area, naturally I thought . . .'

'You thought you'd get pictures of the drama for your magazine,' Vittoria countered.

'Doesn't she wish to photograph me?' the Contessa had asked after Margaret's first visit to the Casa Sanfelice. 'One of the officers gave me a pot of rouge for special occasions. You could do with a little powder yourself, my dear, something to soften the sunburn, it is most unladylike.'

Vittoria occasionally indulged in a fantasy of the typhus fever returning and only killing the Contessa. As it was, the Contessa suffered enough for other reasons: Nonna's kitchen was now full of orphans washing dishes, scrubbing flagstones and gobbling bread from Nina's bakery because Nonna hadn't survived the winter. She now had a new plot of land, not far from where Diavolo was buried.

Vittoria tried not to think about the graveyard. She was here in the hospital for the living, not the dead.

'There's the nurse in charge,' said Margaret. 'Leave this to me. . .' She spoke a few words in English and the nurse promptly marched off, rolling her eyes in exasperation.

'What did you tell her?'

'That Matron wants an extra pair of hands on the far side of the hospital. We won't have long.'

'It won't take long.'

'And remember – no stealing! If you need anything, ask me.'

Vittoria smiled graciously. Chin up, shoulders square, back straight . . . She entered the ward like a queen making a royal inspection. Each bed held a German patient. Some were awake. They smiled or scowled at her depending on their mood. One had his head entirely covered in bandages. Margaret read the chart at the end of the bed and translated for Vittoria.

'His face and body are badly burned from a tank fire. They say he keeps yanking the IV tubes out, trying to die.'

Vittoria calmly tucked the man's hands inside the bed covers and pulled the sheet taut.

'Behave,' she said.

Where was Peter? She found a chart that had his name printed on the top. So he'd made Corporal? By the look of him, it wasn't a fair return for whatever he'd had to do to earn the honour. She paused at the end of his bed. Very little of him showed. The sheet was drawn up to his shoulders and his eyes were still bandaged after surgery on his scalp. There was a piece of shrapnel on the crate at his bedside and a sad, flat space on the bed where his lower left leg should have been. Convenient for footsore visitors to sit.

'You have more lives than a cat,' she said in German. 'Look at you! I told you not to go back.'

She stroked Peter's hand gently. He stirred a little, lost in a far-off dream. Margaret opened the Gladstone bag and reached for her camera.

'You can put *that* away,' said Vittoria in her most imperious Italian. 'That is not why we're here. Get the radio, please. Tune it to a station playing music, not news reports.'

The only news she wanted to hear was that her mama

was released from prison now Rome was liberated by the Allies. As for Papa . . . there was no telling what the news about Papa would be. Auschwitz was thousands of miles away in German territory and the war was far from won yet.

Peter woke. 'Nurse?'

Vittoria snorted.

'Vittoria?' He tried to sit up.

'Leave the bandages, you idiot. They improve your face anyway.'

'Vittoria! Is that you? Are we still in Pompeii? Are we dead?'

She pinched his wrist. 'Does that feel like dead? You're in a hospital on the outskirts of Naples. Quite a nice one if you like being around invalids, which I don't.'

'I can hear . . . is that music? Jazz?' His mouth widened into a smile.

'I thought you might need cheering up.' She was glad he couldn't see her smiling back at him.

He gave a croaky laugh. 'Injured, defeated, captured – why would I need cheering up? I'm only happy the nurses aren't all mean Italian girls like you. Don't hit me!'

She landed a very, very light punch on his chest.

'So, what are the English nurses like?'

He laughed again. 'Strict. Kind. My English isn't so good. *Hello, goodbye, how about a nice cup of tea?* I should learn the language of the country that's conquered me, shouldn't I?' The laugh dwindled. 'How . . . how are you?'

How was she? Tired. Thin. Worn out caring, running Casa Sanfelice. Poorer by four gold coins, spent on the Via Forcella. Strangely happy.

'I am invincible, of course. Zecca says hello by the way, and the other children are fine, except my friend Nina has taken up with a Yankee marine who comes to the bakery and boasts about orange groves in California. I'm ashamed to think of her being sweet on a soldier.'

He gripped her hand more tightly.

'I didn't want to leave you,' he whispered.

There was a pause. She said, 'I'm going now. I'm just wanted to make sure you were still alive.'

'You have to go? I've got something for you. A message, in my diary.'

'You still have that? I suppose you read it when you need to get to sleep, it's so boring?'

'Under my pillow.'

He lay still as she reached forward. His face was very close to hers.

286

The diary was crumpled and battered, rather like its owner.

'What am I looking for?'

'There's a piece of card, the back of cigarette pack.'

She leafed through the photographs slotted into the diary, in particular the shot of Peter and Erich as new recruits, grinning like gold medal winners. Idiots.

'Have you got it?' His hand found her arm. 'Read it.'

'I can't read Latin, you swine!'

'A good incentive for you to learn.'

'*Forsan miseros meliora sequentur.* Pure nonsense.'

'It's Virgil. It means, *For those in misery perhaps better things will follow.* I was hoping things would be better for you . . .'

Vittoria scrunched her eyes up so tears wouldn't come out. 'Look, Margaret!' she suddenly called in Italian. 'Isn't that Vesuvius erupting again?'

Margaret rushed to the window. While the woman's back was turned, Vittoria bent and gave Peter a sweet, deep, heartfelt kiss.

That was her reply to his message.

She tucked his diary into the crook of his arm and fled.

Back in the town centre she steered Margaret towards one of the little cafés soaking up the sun near the blue waters of the bay.

'What will happen to them, the German prisoners? Where will they go?'

Margaret shrugged. 'I don't know. Canada, some of them. Maybe England.'

Vittoria thought about this for a while then, in her best regal tones, she commanded: 'Teach me English!'

The Hero

Richard is coming Richard is coming Richard is coming . . .

This was the beat of my heart as we counted down the final hours.

I asked Mum, 'There won't be any anti-war demos when he gets in, will there?' I could just imagine Samantha Green spitting on anything in uniform just for the fun of it.

Mum went a bit pink but shook her head. 'It's only Richard coming home this time, not the whole regiment. There won't be any fuss.'

No fuss?! Our house was an *orgy* of fuss the day we went to pick Rich up. Everything had been cleaned, tidied, lost, found, mucked about with, messed up and re-tidied. Some distant relatives tried to invite themselves over. Mum told them it was just going to be a quiet time for close family . . . meaning we didn't want to share all the outstandingly delicious food cling-filmed-up in the kitchen. I said it was only fair Gavin should come, as he really wanted to meet Rich. Mum said fine, he could come and join us later in the evening, as long as he could cope with us all being a bit mad.

'Close family' somehow came to mean the Shepherds too, not least because Dr Shepherd made a mean 'fruits of the sea' pasta salad. She was going to hold the fort with her husband while we went to collect Rich from his base and bring him home.

'Don't be surprised if your brother is a little different from how you remember,' Mr Shepherd told me before we set off. 'He's seen things . . . done things . . .'

I wanted to say, it's all right, I understand, only I didn't. Neither did Craig. All Mum knew was that Rich had been discharged from the army hospital – he'd told us absolutely not to visit – but he'd need to keep going back for some kind of physiotherapy.

'That's OK,' said Craig. 'Tariq's going to need physio for the knee he knackered at cross-country the other day.'

Mum didn't look convinced. 'I must say, your brother's been very stubborn the few times we've actually spoken on the phone. I wish he'd just tell me what happened. All we know is his vehicle hit a roadside mine. He says he's fine, but . . . Never mind. Don't worry, you two. He's back in one piece and that's all that matters.'

Well, technically, that wasn't strictly true. Rich wasn't exactly in one piece. He'd left part of his body behind in Afghanistan. When we got past security at the base and finally met him in some random room, we straightaway saw that half of one leg was missing.

Rich leaped up to say hello, balanced on a set of crutches.

'Oh my God . . .' Mum put her hand over her mouth. 'Richard – you never said. Your leg! You poor thing!'

Me and Craig just stared at the long bit of empty space where his shin and foot should've been. The end of his trouser was pinned up under the stump.

Rich joked, 'Just a scratch!' Balancing on one crutch he opened his arms. 'Don't I get a welcome home hug?'

A hug? He got a ton of them, Mum first, then me and Craig. We're not an especially huggy family usually. It was strange but nice to give Rich a good old squish. He felt strong and healthy, apart from the missing bit.

'Why didn't you tell me!' Mum wailed when she'd done sniffing back tears. She was all over him, crying and smiling at the same time. I stood there like a complete lemon, happy and scared.

'No big deal,' said Rich. 'Could've been worse.' His face went very white.

Mum must've been thinking, yeah it could've been worse, you could've been killed out there.

I know that's exactly what was going through my mind.

'Do you need to sit down?' I asked.

'I'm fine! Shall we make a move?'

Craig wanted to help lift Rich's kitbag but it was way too heavy. Rich heaved it up and slung it over one shoulder, then tackled his crutches again.

'Stop staring at me like I'm some sort of freak. I told you I'm fine. You don't have to be on eggshells round me. Except don't ask me to drive.'

He didn't quite look like the Richard I remembered, not just because of the obvious injury or the fact he was a few months older. If anything, he seemed bigger than before, and louder. He joked practically non-stop in the car and said loads of inane things like, *Wow, the supermarket's still open*, or, *I see they haven't burned the school down yet.*

Craig started asking him all sorts of war-ish questions. That's when Rich pretty much clammed up.

'Oh you don't want to know about that stuff,' he said.

Dr and Mr Shepherd kept in the background when we arrived. They stood in a corner of our kitchen holding hands.

Rich seemed too big for the house. He was kind of

292

gruff, too. The glorious feast got a quick, 'Nice spread,' then he was battling with his crutches in a bid to liberate beer from the fridge. Not one beer – all of them. We drank to his safe return and started on the food.

I found myself blabbing about school and Gavin and things. Rich listened, or tried to. His eyes kept wandering round the kitchen, like it was somewhere he didn't quite recognise. His mobile buzzed. He answered it and said something about maybe meeting a few of his old mates at the pub. Mum said wouldn't it be better to go another night. Rich said fine, it was no big deal, and made what looked like a big effort to look jolly again.

Rich ended up talking to Mr Shepherd. I watched them for a bit. Just two people chatting, right? Wrong! Time to unmuddle things. Time to test my new theory. (Or, time to look like a complete loon because I'd guessed wrong.)

'You two obviously have a lot to talk about, both being paratroopers,' I said loudly.

'Who's a paratrooper?' Craig butted in.

'Ah,' said Dr Shepherd slowly. 'You know.'

'Know what?' echoed Craig. I couldn't help it, I had to hug him. 'Get off me, you psycho! Know *what*?'

'About Peter Schäfer,' I said.

Mr Shepherd looked a bit embarrassed. Rich, Mum and Craig looked totally confused. For once I'd done

293

something remarkable. I'd surprised them.

'It was in the dictionary,' I said. 'It just needed a bit of deduction and brainpower. *Schäfer* is the German word for *shepherd*, right?'

Dr Shepherd clapped her hands, delighted. '*Molto bene!* Very clever! Shepherd in English, Schäfer in German. It was best to change the name when staying in England after the war.'

Mr Shepherd – *Mr Schäfer* – gave a shy smile. 'Excuse my hesitation to explain I was a prisoner of war in England. Not everyone is . . . understanding.'

Craig's eyeballs finally receded into their sockets.

'You have got to be joking,' he spluttered. 'You can't be Peter Schäfer, you're *old*!'

'I wasn't always,' came Mr Shepherd's energetic reply. 'One time I was ready to compete in the Olympics.'

Mum said, 'Craig's done nothing but talk about Peter Schäfer since he met you. I hadn't realised . . . Well, I suppose he hadn't either. I never knew we were living next door to . . . to a German veteran.'

There was a *very* awkward pause while she tried to work out if she should be outraged or shocked or offended. Then she sighed and said, 'My father worked on the railways during the war, a reserved occupation. He always felt he missed out on something, shirked his duty,

I don't know. He said the men who fought were heroes.'

Mr Shepherd shook his head.

'They gave me a medal for my part in the war, but I say the best men died. I never felt like a hero, not when the fighting started. I just felt scared.'

Did I imagine it, or was there a fleeting look of relief on Rich's face when he heard that? Relief and understanding.

Mum couldn't stop talking to cover up her embarrassment. Or maybe she was being sociable. I can't tell the difference.

'So you've been in England all this time? You didn't go back to Germany when you were released from . . . prison camp, wherever it was you were?'

He said, 'I worked on a farm, not too far from here in fact. No, I did not go back. I was reluctant to be in Germany when I learned about certain aspects of the war – the death camps, mainly, Auschwitz and so on. Besides, I liked England. The people were kind, like the Italians.'

Mum looked at Dr Shepherd. 'Your family are Italian? Where on earth did you two meet?'

Dr Shepherd didn't mention Naples or Italy. She said she'd learned English, saved up and come to England after the war, with one suitcase, a dog called Winston and plans to study at university.

'After the war I found out where Peter was working and

took a train. There was no telephone so I walked from the station to find his farm. He was cycling back from work.'

'I nearly fell off my bicycle to see Vicky there in the lane, so smart. So beautiful.'

'Oh be quiet about that.'

Mr Shepherd grinned. 'I made her marry me quickly before she changed her mind. I couldn't wait. We spent all our money on books, music and whatever food we could afford. Food for the dog, mostly! In my spare time I joined with other servicemen to start a jazz band.'

Rich stuck his hand in the air to interrupt. One crutch clattered to the floor. 'Hold up, hold up . . . I'm missing stuff here. You're one of the guys from the Silver Eagles? We *loved* that CD you sent out to us! Stumpy especially . . .' His face twisted and his lips went thin. He rallied. 'You mean you're the *Fallschirmjäger* guy Craig wrote about? It's an honour to meet you, sir.' And he stuck his hand out to shake Mr Shepherd's.

Everyone seemed to let out their breath at the same time – spontaneous relaxation. After that Rich nattered away quite happily with Mr S, one soldier to another. I was just glad to see him halfway to normal.

Out of the corner of my eye I spotted Dr Shepherd filching prawns from the dregs of the pasta salad. She was so light-fingered. Vittoria Venafro, Queen of Thieves! She winked at me. Old loon. I was too shy to ask all the things I wanted to know.

Raised voices.

Rich's mood had switched again. He was battering a beer can flat on the table and scowling at Mr Shepherd.

'Go back there? *Of course* I want to get back to my mates – what's left of them. But how the hell can I finish my tour with half my leg blown off? No disrespect, but it doesn't matter how good I was at the job or how much I liked it, that's all over now, isn't it? I'm out on the scrap heap. Candidate for a dull desk job. One of those cripples nice people at the pool complain about because seeing leg stumps puts them off their swim!'

Dr Shepherd cut through the shocked silence that followed. '*Stupidotto!* I do not understand this obsession with returning to war, Richard Cooper, but you should not allow one wound to stop you doing what you want.'

'One wound? Lady, I've only got one *leg*!'

'That's *Doctor* Lady to you, and yes, I do not wear glasses, I can see you have an inconvenience. It never stopped my husband. Why should it stop you? Put another leg on! Peter, show them, show them.'

Mr Shepherd quietly lifted his left trouser leg. Sure enough, above the sock there was a metal rod.

'Caught by a mortar at Monte Cassino,' he explained.

'I got a wooden leg first. These days they have such prosthetics! I watch the athletes run at the Paralympics and wish such things had been invented when I was younger.'

Rich deflated. 'Jesus. I'm sorry. I didn't realise. Wow.'

'You see!' Dr Shepherd exclaimed triumphantly. 'A leg blown off, just like yours, and he still got off his bike and ran down the lane when he saw me arrive that day in spring, after the war.' She smiled at her hubby, going off on one of her rambling memories. 'You were in those terrible, how do you say . . . ?'

Mr Shepherd smiled a gentle smile. 'Corduroy overalls.'

'*Davvero*, and me with a new dress and shoes.'

'And short hair!'

'What did you expect? A glamour model? I was a businesswoman then, running a hotel in Naples.'

'God help the guests!' laughed her husband, then, at that moment, he must've swallowed a prawn wrong, because half his face seemed to slide downward and his hand flew out to grab whatever was nearest . . . my brother Rich . . . who caught and held him till the ambulance came.

It Must Be Returned

Peter Robert Schäfer died in his wife's arms one sunny morning in May.

The stroke he suffered while in our kitchen weakened him but it didn't finish him off. He still had the end of winter and most of spring to enjoy. I'd never watched anyone dying before. You want to hold them back and stop them slipping away. You can't. You think, how can being alive just *end*? It does.

Craig cried his heart out when it finally happened. I guess I did too. Call me stupid, but I was also crying for Dad, even though I'd never known him. Maybe *because* I'd never known him.

I don't know if Dr Shepherd cried. She refused to have anything to do with a funeral, as if that would somehow make her husband less dead.

Mum made arrangements for a service at the local crematorium. 'The Shepherds are as good as family now,' she said.

We all went to the funeral, thinking we'd be the only ones there, but the place was pretty full, mostly old people or fans of the Silver Eagles, including Gavin and his dad, who said hello-nice-to-meet-you-finally. Then the chapel doors opened for Mr Shepherd's coffin, and who should be carrying it in but six British paras, all in tiptop shiny uniforms, and who should be the tallest and strongest of those paras? Our brother Rich, that's who, two trouser legs right down to his glossy black boots.

He hadn't said anything about getting time off for the funeral, or about being able to walk on his new fake leg, the sneaky pig. He kept his eyes front as they slow-marched, but I swear he winked at me, as if to say: look, no crutches!

It was bizarre, seeing the British paras honouring a dead German, someone who'd've been their enemy a few decades ago. Bizarre but not exactly *wrong*. He was another fallen soldier to them, a kind of comrade.

I cried. I liked Mr Shepherd being alive, even if he was old and ill. I also cried because I knew Dr Shepherd would be sad. I went to see her after the service. She'd stayed in bed at home, saying she couldn't bear to see so many people wearing black. It was the first time I'd noticed how old she was, not just white-haired and bony – *old*. She turned her head from me.

'Always I am left alone. First my Peter dies, then it will be Winnie.'

'You said you always get another Winston when one dog dies.'

'Yes, yes, we have had a dog called Winston since 1943 but I will not choose another one now. Who will look after it when I have crossed the *pomerium* to the other side?'

'We will! Craig's desperate for a puppy. We'll get one from animal rescue.'

'It will only die too. It's all death in the end. You love people and you lose them.'

'Sometimes you find them. Rich wasn't dead – he came home!'

She hesitated. 'That is true. My father too, I lost him but he came home. He was arrested as a Jew. Italian Jews were put on trains to Auschwitz – have you heard of it? You know of the Holocaust, yes? Perhaps the darkest shadow of the war, I think. It was Margaret Bentley-Wyke who found him, *che milagro*! A miracle! She was taking photographs in a liberated concentration camp in 1945, you see – Bergen Belsen, where Anne Frank was too – and then she saw the name Vittorio Venafro on a list of survivors who'd been transported to Belsen from Auschwitz. So I had my papa again after the war, Mama too. How funny it was. All that time I wanted them home to take care of me and when they came I wasn't a baby any more. I wanted to find my own way in the world.'

'So you came to England to find Peter? That's so romantic.'

Of all the stupid idiots in the world, I'm the biggest. Fancy talking about her husband when he was only just dead!

She didn't seem to mind – huge relief.

'Oh, he was trouble, that boy,' she said with a smile. 'But very handsome trouble, and gentle in his own way. We took care of each other.'

She stroked my hand. Hers was so fine and weak.

'Shall I put the kettle on?' I asked.

'Ask Nonna, she will bring a tray up.'

'Nonna?'

'The servant!'

'There aren't any servants . . .'

'Not now! Back in Naples. But of course, I remember. Nonna died. One of the children will bring us tea instead. So many orphans after the war! The Contessa hid in her bedroom! They were running up and down the stairs and jumping on the beds when they were supposed to be making them. Of course, when other places struggled to get food and supplies somehow Hotel Sanfelice always had enough. Yes, yes, *La Regina degli Ladroni*, they called me still. Queen of Thieves. But I didn't want that for ever. When I came to marry Peter they all found work and homes. Nina Dragone, my friend, made me this quilt.'

She plucked at the bedcover with trembling fingers.

'She sent it all the way from California when she was married. This square here, this is a piece from her wedding dress. These are from tablecloths we made into clothes for the orphans. So many memories sewn into the cloth. It stops them falling out of my brain. This green velvet, so faded now, this I wore the first time I saw Peter at the marina café one sunny morning in *Napoli* . . .'

Her words broke and she started to cry.

I felt awful, just watching, not knowing what to do or say. There was no escaping the large expanse of empty bed where her husband had once slept.

She pulled herself together a bit.

'So, Peter's funeral is on May nineteenth. The Germans lost at Monte Cassino yesterday, years ago, did you know? The Allies had a sad victory there after so many months of suffering and dying. Fetch my things, I will show you.'

303

I got her bundle of memories and she spread them over the quilt, touching them one by one. The green insignia, the piece of pumice, the fragment of shrapnel. The photo of two paratroopers. When she smoothed out the crumpled newspaper I could read the headlines and report:

Daily Mail
For King and Empire
Friday, 19th May, 1944

CASSINO GARRISON CRACK:
MASS SURRENDER.
The White Flag Waved on Monastery Hill

Cassino is ours. The last Germans to surrender, blinking in the unaccustomed sunlight, with dirty chalk-white faces from their long siege in the underground dug-outs and tunnels, were being marched out early this morning. It was obvious that the paratroops left in Cassino and the Monastery were in a hopeless position. At nine o'clock the first white flag fluttered in the ruins. Shortly afterwards ten Poles began to advance on the Monastery but they met with no resistance –

all the fight had been knocked out of Hitler's
tough and arrogant parachute division.

She touched the yellowing paper and murmured, 'Pink
roses grew among the wrecked tanks, and poppies,
poppies everywhere, like a garden of death. *Allora*, that is
all done now. And Peter, he had more life than a soldier
on Monte Cassino had any right to expect, believe me.
Now, go to the top drawer, no, the other one. Open it.
Take the envelope. There, you see, *i biglietti*, for August.
Your mother understands, she has agreed.'

I went pink. Three tickets to Rome. It hadn't all
been the ramblings of a demented mind. She really meant
us to go.

'One for you, two for your brothers.'

'Rich is going? Not you?'

'I will not go anywhere again. Richard was a friend to
Peter these last months. He knows what death is now. He
has seen it. He has his own pain to blow away over the
sea. He will know how to help. Now leave me alone. I
want to be unhappy.'

She did rally a bit, come August. I walked with her to
the war memorial the day before the flight. We sat
together on a park bench looking at the old wreaths. She
was very thin. She took hold of my arm. Her hand was

305

shaking, her voice was weak.

'Such a big moon,' she murmured, even though it was broad daylight. 'And colder than you would expect in August. Always I intended to go myself but now you must go to Herculaneum beach and tell him, if you can find him. Do not be late.'

'Tell who what?'

She leaned close and whispered in my ear. Then, just to show she wasn't out of practice, she stole my purse and I never even noticed till she handed it back, fat with euros to spend.

'*Ciao*,' she said softly. '*Buon viaggio*.'

The airport, the flight, the first sight of Rome's red roofs and tall green pines . . . it was all so strange and exotic. I just kept turning my face to the sun and let Rich bundle me into trains. Was this what it was like, *doing* things, going out into life? I liked it! Would've liked it more if I didn't have a terrible sense of dread weighing me down.

First we went to Cassino.

Craig and Rich jabbered on about all the battles and made me visit places Peter would have been. It was all too weird, seeing a modern town on a beautiful day, and a mountain covered in wild flowers. How could there have been a war here? There were lads my age skateboarding on the war memorial in the town centre.

Rich hired a car and drove us up zigzag hairpin bends to the monastery. The strangest thing of all was that the whole thing was still there, rebuilt after the war.

'Not much point in bombing it then,' I said.

'That sign over the door is original,' Craig said, reading the guidebook.

It was a big red sign that just said PAX.

I liked the monastery crypt best. It was gold and shiny with mosaic peacocks, eagles and flowers. When I came out into the sunshine again, we leaned over a stone balcony to be dazzled by the view of the wide valley. Craig announced, 'Peter's leg was blown off somewhere out there.'

I squinted, half expecting to see a foot in a German boot, still lying around. Idiot! I couldn't help glancing at Richard's leg. He wore long trousers even though it was a baking hot day, not wanting anyone to see the fake leg. Fair enough. I guessed he was wondering what Monte Cassino would be like to defend or attack.

There was a big graveyard for Polish soldiers nearby with hundreds of white crosses. The German war graves were on a mountain slope a little way out of town. Rich led us along quiet paths, scanning the rows and rows of white headstones. Six Germans buried in each grave; six names on each marker, except where the names weren't known, then they were just *Ein Deutscher Soldat*. A German soldier. I guess some of the graves must've held some German kid's father though I don't suppose many German relatives would've been welcome in Italy after the war, coming to grieve for the enemy. It was nice the cemetery was looked after at least.

Then we found the one we'd been looking for.

Stabsgefr. Erich Bergen
10.10.24–15.3.44

Rich brushed away green leaves and let Craig bury a small medal with a faded ribbon in the dry soil. Peter Schäfer's Iron Cross, Second Class.

I stood there, all out of place. We'd never known Erich, why was Rich staying so long at the grave? Because he was crying, that's why. My eyes filled too, just from watching. It's scary seeing someone big and strong upset.

Rich tried to pull himself together.

'Sorry. Man! I thought I'd got my head straight about Stumpy.' He wiped his face on his sleeve. 'The stupid gimp lost more than his leg when we drove over that mine. He . . . There was nothing I could do. He just lay there, not moving. Sorry. I'm fine. I just . . . Stumpy was a top bloke, a real good mate.'

'Why are you so desperate to go back and fight then?' I challenged.

He shrugged the question off.

'Come on,' he said. 'We'll go to the Allied graveyard.'

The next big cemetery pretty much finished me off – so many gravestones, so many names, all nestling in green grass and perfumed roses. So many dead, and all for that great big monastery still high on the mountain top, looking down, indifferent.

When I looked up from the lines of white grave slabs and stared at Monastery Hill it seemed as if the rocky slopes were actually made up of row on row of graves too, now turning a dull grey-orange in the twilight.

The sun set. The air cooled. Time was running out. We had to get to Naples.

On the Beach

There really is a huge volcano dominating the Bay of Naples. You read about it, you see the pictures, but it's not the same.

'Imagine that monster blowing its top off,' Craig whistled when Vesuvius first came into view. He made exuberant eruption noises until Rich and I glared him into submission. It did get me thinking, though, about how life can explode when you least expect it, even if things look normal. That's scary . . . and exciting.

Naples itself didn't look like the Dark Ages any more, whatever the guidebooks said. There were still plenty of crumbly buildings in between the new office blocks plus so much graffiti the artists must get repetitive strain injury from all the spray-painting.

Walking into Hotel Sanfelice was like walking into

someone else's life. There was an eagle carved in the stone over the massive wooden door where Dr Shepherd said Peter had first come knocking the day she stole his diary. (*In this sign victorious.*) There were marble steps in the hall, now covered in carpet. There was an old piano in the big sitting room and a mirror with lots of eagles and other heraldic stuff. There were framed photos of children on the wall of my bedroom – grinning, gurning, gorgeous faces. I thought of Queen Vittoria looking after them all, a legend in her own time.

Craig rolled round the door frame.

'Rich says a man from the hotel will drive us to Herculaneum, except they call it Ercolano, even though the town's actually called Resina. Don't ask me why. Apparently it's a bit of a rough area so you're not to wear any blingy jewellery or carry money. I'm taking the *Fallschirmjäger* knife Mr Shepherd gave me.'

'Right, I'll hide behind you then.'

There'd be time to climb the volcano. Time to wander round Pompeii and see the city of Herculaneum. Now it was twilight on August twenty-fourth. Time to go to the beach.

There was no moon, just faint prickles of starlight above the light pollution of the bay. Vesuvius spread across the night sky, flat-topped and quiet ever since the last eruption in 1944. They said it was due to blow again, any time. Surely not tonight of all nights? Well, anything could happen, or probably nothing. My vote was for nothing.

Our driver dimmed his headlights and pointed to a narrow alleyway. 'The sea is there,' he said. 'Go down, go right, cross the wall, you are there. I wait for you here, when you come back.'

If we come back, I thought.

At least we had Rich with us. He tucked some sort of bundle in his arm, something he'd been carrying all the way from England – probably illegally judging by the relief on his face when our baggage appeared in Rome airport without interrogation. He went down the alley first. It stank of burst rubbish bags and worse. Craig and I just followed.

'Are you sure . . . ?' I started to say.

Rich replied, 'It's fine. This sort of thing's a piece of cake for me, remember.'

Oh that was a good idea – make me think about being in a war zone, with snipers pointing rifles through cracks in the walls and mines underfoot.

Somewhere in the night a baby cried and a television gabbled. I smelled the sea just as I saw it, dark and restless.

Now what?

Rich opened his bundle and took out a wooden box. He opened the lid. The box was full of pale grey-white ash. Seeing it, I felt shaky all over.

Rich hesitated.

'It's all right,' I said, surprising myself even. 'I'll do it.' Suddenly I understood what Dr Shepherd had been telling me all along.

Something was taken, it must be returned.

Craig's voice was squeaky. 'You're going to scatter Peter Schäfer's ashes in the sea?'

I nodded. 'Dr Shepherd was always saying life's only borrowed, that you have to give it back. If she asked Rich to bring Peter here, well, this is what she wanted us to do next, I'm sure of it.'

The ashes were surprisingly soft and light. I was careful to stand with the breeze at my back as I lifted the box and shook it to let the flakes waft out. Rich was speaking but I couldn't hear what he said. A soldier's prayer? Words for his mate Stumpy?

I stood watching ash settle on the gentle water until something new caught my attention. Something moving further along the beach, just between

313

shadow and uncertainty.

I took a few hesitant steps across the rocks and rusty junk littering the seashore.

Was someone there?

I heard nothing but the idle slap of seawater.

The air was very grey. Everything seemed to pause, even the beats of my heart.

'Hello?'

Did I speak out loud? I don't know. Did I hear a reply?

Ave, said the breeze. *Hail and well met.*

I breathed again, barely.

'Are you there?'

Are you there? came the mocking echo.

'I'm here. Where are you?'

Here.

Then I saw him. A man I didn't believe in. A soldier with a sword hanging from his belt. He was standing staring out to sea, so grey he almost wasn't there.

'I . . . I've got a message for you. Vittoria sent me.'

At that he turned. His eyes were too deep to look at for long.

'It's not a long message. I mean, she didn't say to tell you about how she is, or Peter, or all the children.'

Ah . . . they lived. They did not die screaming.

I swallowed. 'No one died, except Peter, eventually.'

314

So tell me your message.

Deep breaths.

'Just one word, that's all she said. One word.'

One word?

'It was . . . she said . . . at least I think she meant you . . . She just said *grazie*. Thank you.'

The man shivered as the word blew through him. I held out my hand, to show him his gold coin. He didn't want it. For a moment I felt poised on the edge of life, wavering, wavering, drifting, falling, then . . .

'Denise!' Craig was calling me.

I said, 'I'm right here! Don't panic!'

He ran over. 'It's all done now, isn't it? We can tell Dr Shepherd when we get home.'

I shook my head and looked along the beach.

'Actually, I don't think she'll be there.'

Just for a moment I saw them one last time – the limping soldier, the young German and the tall girl with glossy hair, all leaving together, crossing that faint grey line between life and death, then . . . gone.

I gazed out over the dark blue bay as midnight tipped us into the twenty-fifth of August and the start of a new day.

Author's Note

Burning Mountain is a fictional story. Much of it is also true.

What amazed me most about writing this story is how little I had to make up. Every time I wondered if I was stretching credibility too far, new facts and fables came to light, showing my imagination wasn't running so wild after all. Troops massing for battle in 1944 had front-row seats for the eruption of Vesuvius. Roman treasures were hoarded at Monte Cassino. Music lovers meeting at the sweaty *Cavern* bar in Liverpool really could see The Beatles as warm-up act for a *Fallschirmjäger* soldier jazz player.

Paratroopers, pickpockets, hallucinations, hell-in-paradise – the real stories of wartime Italy are remarkable and moving, as are reports constantly emerging from war zones around the world now.

Gaius Justinius Aquila, in truth, has no name, but a soldier's skeleton was found on the old Roman beach at Herculaneum, complete with a sword and a pouch of coins . . .

My thanks go to Kay and Roberto in Italy who provided heartfelt historical tours, hospitality, schnapps and ice cream.

Another stunning story by L.J. Adlington

THE DIARY OF PELLY D

For Pelly D, her life stretches ahead, filled with glorious possibilities. But young building worker, Toni V, has just found her diary. Buried in a water can. In the rubble of a construction site. And with it, there's a note:

DIG, DIG EVERYWHERE.

It's against all the rules – he should just hand it in to the Supervisor – but Toni V is curious and he begins to read . . .

Buried beneath the sassy voice of a girl he's never met, he begins to sense another more sinister truth unfolding.

Another stunning story by L.J. Adlington

CHERRY HEAVEN

i remember the last birthday i ever had was when i
got shot instead of presents
where i come from remembering's Against the Rules
you only find out what the rules are when you
break them.

i remember me

i'm Luka

DON'T ANY OF YOU GET IN MY WAY

Kat and Tanka are looking for a bright new future
far from the bullet holes and bomb craters of the
war in the cities that tore their parents away.

A fresh start on the New Frontier.

A beautiful new home – Cherry Heaven.

Peace. Happiness.

No shadows.

But softly, secretly, shadows are creeping towards
them . . .

Another stunning story by L.J. Adlington

THE GLITTERING EYE

Shabti wakes in a barley field.
No past
No memories.
No escape from a vicious master and dogs set to rip the flesh off his bones.

Amy arrives in Egypt to join her archaeologist father. Beyond the River Nile's safe shores lies the desert. Vast red cliffs, rocks, sky. Everywhere, the unblinking eye of the sun. And tombs, unearthed, opened, entered . . .

Why, Amy wonders, do people always have to dig up things that are best left buried?

THE CARBON DIARIES 2015
by Saci Lloyd

Shortlisted for the 2008 Costa Children's Book Award

It's 2015 and the UK is the first nation to introduce carbon dioxide rations in a drastic bid to cut greenhouse gas emissions.

As her family spirals rapidly out of control, Laura Brown chronicles the first year of rationing with scathing abandon.

Will her mother become one with her inner wolf? Does her father love the pig more than her? Can her band, the *dirty angels*, make it big? And most importantly, will Ravi Datta ever love her?

In these dark days, Laura deals with the issues that really matter: love, floods and pigs.

THE CARBON DIARIES 2017
by Saci Lloyd

The must-read sequel to the Costa-shortlisted
The Carbon Diaries 2015.

It's 2017 and London is a city on the edge, fighting for survival in the new carbon rationing era. As ever, Laura Brown is right on the front line, charting events with acerbic wit as Europe descends into student revolt, strikes and a bitter water war.

These are revolutionary times, and it's down to Laura to deal with the big stuff – how to keep her love life under control, her parents chilled out, and that dream of world domination with her band, the *dirty angels*, alive.